Henry Hall

Ethan Allen

The Robin Hood of Vermont

Henry Hall

Ethan Allen
The Robin Hood of Vermont

ISBN/EAN: 9783337361945

Printed in Europe, USA, Canada, Australia, Japan

Cover: Foto ©Andreas Hilbeck / pixelio.de

More available books at **www.hansebooks.com**

ETHAN ALLEN

The Robin Hood of Vermont

BY

HENRY HALL

NEW YORK
D. APPLETON AND COMPANY
1895

PREFACE.

AT the time of the death of Mr. Henry Hall, in 1889, the manuscript for this volume consisted of finished fragments and many notes. It was left in the hands of his daughters to complete. The purpose of the author was to make a fuller life of Allen than has been written, and singling him from that cluster of sturdy patriots in the New Hampshire Grants, to make plain the vivid personality of a Vermont hero to the younger generations. Mr. Hall's well-known habit of accuracy and painstaking investigation must be the guaranty that this "Life" is worthy of a place among the volumes of the history of our nation.

HENRIETTA HALL BOARDMAN.

CONTENTS.

CHAPTER VI.

CHAPTER VII.

CHAPTER VIII.

CHAPTER IX.

CHAPTER X.

CHAPTER XVI.

CHAPTER XVII.

CHAPTER XVIII.

ETHAN ALLEN.

CHAPTER I.

ETHAN ALLEN is the Robin Hood of Vermont. As Robin Hood's life was an Anglo-Saxon protest against Norman despotism, so Allen's life was a protest against domestic robbery and foreign tyranny. As Sherwood Forest was the rendezvous of the gallant and chivalrous Robin Hood, so the Green Mountains were the home of the dauntless and high-minded Ethan Allen. As Robin Hood, in Scott's "Ivanhoe," so does Allen, in Thompson's "Green Mountain Boys," win our admiration. Although never a citizen of the United States, he is one of the heroes of the state and the nation; one of those whose names the people will not willingly let die. History and tradition, song and story, sculpture, engraving, and photography alike blazon his memory from ocean to ocean. The librarian of the great library at Worcester, Massachusetts, told Colonel Higginson that the book most read was Daniel P. Thompson's "Green Mountain Boys." Already one centennial celebration of the capture of Ticonderoga has been celebrated. Who can tell how many future anniversaries of that capture our nation will live to see! Another reason for refreshing our memories with the history of Allen is the bitterness with which he is attacked. He has been accused of ignorance, weakness of mind, cowardice, infidelity, and atheism. Among his assailants have been the president of a college, a clergyman, editors, contributors to magazines and newspapers, and even a local historian among a variety of writers of greater or less prominence. If Vermont is careful of her own fame, well does it become the people to know whether Ethan Allen was a hero or a humbug.

Arnold calls history the vast Mississippi of falsehood. The untruths that have been published about Allen during the last hundred and fifteen years might not fill and overflow the Ohio branch of such a Mississippi, but

they would make a lively rivulet run until it
was dammed by its own silt. The late Benjamin Disraeli, Lord Beaconsfield, fought a
duel with Daniel O'Connell, because O'Connell
declared it to be his belief that Disraeli was
a lineal descendant of the impenitent thief on
the Cross. Perhaps the libellers of Allen are
descended from the Yorkers whom he stamped
so ignominiously with the beech seal. The
fierce light of publicity perhaps never beat
upon a throne more sharply than for more than
a hundred years it has beat upon Ethan Allen.
His patriotism, courage, religious belief, and
general character have been travestied and
caricatured until now the real man has to be
dug up from heaps of untruthful rubbish, as
the peerless Apollo Belvidere was dug in the
days of Columbus from the ruins of classic
Antium.

Discrepancies exist even in regard to his
age. On the stone tablet over his grave his
age is given as fifty years. Thompson said his
age was fifty-two. At the unveiling of his
statue, he was called thirty-eight years old
when Ticonderoga was taken. These three
statements are erroneous, and, strange to say,
Burlington is responsible for them all. Bur-

lington, the Athens of Vermont, the town wherein rest his ashes, the town wherein most of the last two years of his life were passed, and the town that has done most to honor his memory.

However humiliating it may be to state pride, it is probable that the Allens, centuries ago, were no more respectable than the ancestors of Queen Victoria and the oldest British peers. The different ways of spelling the name, Alleyn, Alain, Allein, and Allen, seem to indicate a Norman origin. George Allen, professor in the University of Pennsylvania, says that Alain had command of the rear of William the Conqueror's army at the battle of Hastings in 1066.

Joseph Allen, the father of Ethan, comes to the surface of history about the year 1720, one year after the death of Addison and the first publication of "Robinson Crusoe," in the town of Coventry, in Eastern Connecticut, twenty miles east of Hartford. When he first appears to us he is a minor and an orphan. His widowed mother, Mercy, has several children, one of them of age. Their first recorded act is emigration fifty miles westward to Litchfield, famous for its scenery and ancient elms,

located between the Naugatuck and the She-
paug rivers, on the Green and Taconic mountain ranges; famous also as the place where
the first American ladies' seminary was located, and most famous of all for its renowned
law-school, begun over a century ago by
Judge Tapping Reeve and continued by Judge
James Gould. Chief Justice John Pierpoint and
United States Senator S. S. Phelps were among
its notable pupils. The widow, Mercy Allen,
died in Litchfield, February 5, 1728. Her son
Joseph bought one-third of her real estate.
Within five years he sold two tracts, of 100
acres each, and fourteen years after his mother's death he sold the residue as wild land.
On March 11, 1737, Joseph Allen was married
to Mary Baker, daughter of John Baker, of
Woodbury, sister of Remember Baker, who
was father of the Remember Baker that came
to Vermont. Thus Ethan Allen and Remember Baker were cousins.

Ethan Allen was born January 10, 1737,
and died February 21, 1789, and consequently
he has been said to have been fifty-two years,
one month and two days old. In fact, he was
fifty-one years, one month and two days old.
The year 1737 terminated March 24. Had it

closed December 31, Allen would have been born in 1738. The first day of the year was March 25 until 1752 in England and her colonies. In 1751 the British Parliament changed New Year's Day from March 25 to January 1. The year 1751 had no January, no February, and only seven days of March. Allen was thirteen years old in 1750, and was fourteen years old in 1752.

The year 1738 gave birth to three honest men—Ethan Allen, George III., and Benjamin West. In 1738 George Washington was six years old, John Adams three years old, John Stark ten years old, Israel Putnam twenty years old. Seth Warner and Jefferson were born five years later. In that year no claim had ever been made to Vermont by New York or New Hampshire. No one had ever questioned the right of Massachusetts to the English part of Vermont. New Hampshire was bounded on the west by the Merrimac. Colden, the surveyor-general of New York, in an official report bounded New York on the east by Connecticut and Massachusetts, on the north by Lake Ontario and Canada; Canada occupying Crown Point and Chimney Point.

If by waving a magician's wand the English-American colonies on the Atlantic slope, as they existed in 1738, could pass before us, wherein would the tableau differ from that of to-day? West of the Alleghanies there were the Indians and the French. On the north were 50,000 prosperous French, farmers chiefly along the valley of the St. Lawrence from Montreal to Quebec. On the east, Acadie, including Nova Scotia, New Brunswick, and a part of Maine, was Scotch. Florida was Spanish. From Georgia to Maine were 1,500,-000 English-Americans and 400,000 African-Americans. The colony of New York had a population of 60,100. New Hampshire, consisting of a few thousand settlers, was located north and east of the Merrimac, and had a legislature of its own, but no governor. Massachusetts, with its charters from James I. and Charles I., claimed the country to the Pacific Ocean, and exercised ownership between the Merrimac and Connecticut and west of the Connecticut, without a breath of opposition from any mortal. Massachusetts had sold land as her own which she found to be in Connecticut, and she paid that state for it by granting her many thousand acres in three of the southeast-

ern townships of Vermont. She built and sus-
tained a fort in Brattleboro', kept a garrison
there with a salaried chaplain, salaried resident
Indian commissioner, and she established a
store supplied with provisions, groceries, and
goods suitable for trade with frontiersmen and
the Indians of Canada. Bartering was actively
carried on along the Connecticut River, Black
River, Otter Creek, and Lake Champlain. In
1737 a solemn ratification of the old treaty occurred there; speeches were made, presents
given, and the healths of George II. and Governor Belcher, of Massachusetts, were duly drunk.
There was no Anglo-Saxon settlement in Vermont outside of Brattleboro'. In Pownal were
a few families of Dutch squatters. The Indian
village of St. Francis, midway between Montreal and Quebec, peopled partly by New England refugees from King Philip's war of 1676,
exercised supreme control over northeastern
Vermont.

In all the land were only three colleges:
Harvard, one hundred and two years old,
Yale, thirty-seven, and William and Mary,
forty-five.

Ethan Allen had five brothers, Heman,
Heber, Levi, Zimri, and Ira, and two sisters,

Lydia and Lucy.   Of all our early heroes, few
glide before us with a statelier step or more
beneficent mien than Heman Allen, the oldest brother of Ethan.   Born in Cornwall, Connecticut, October 15, 1740, dying in Salisbury,
Connecticut, May 18, 1778, his life of thirty-
seven and a half years was like that of the
Chevalier Bayard, without fear and without
reproach.   A man of affairs, a merchant and
a soldier, a politician and a land-owner, a
diplomat and a statesman, he was capable, intelligent, honest, earnest, and true.   But fifteen
years old when his father died, he was early engaged in trade at Salisbury.   His home became
the home of his widowed mother and her large
family.   Salisbury was his home and probably
his legal residence, although he represented
Rutland and Colchester in the Vermont Conventions, and was sent to Congress by Dorset.

Heber was the first town clerk of Poultney.

Ira was able, shrewd, and gentlemanly; a
land surveyor and speculator, a lieutenant in
Warner's regiment, a member of all the conventions of 1776 and 1777, of the Councils of
Safety and of the State Council; state treasurer, surveyor-general, author of a " History
of " Vermont, and of various official papers and

political pamphlets. In 1796 he bought, in France," twenty-four brass cannon and twenty thousand muskets, ostensibly for the Vermont militia, which were seized by the English. After a lawsuit of seven or eight years he regained them, but the expense beggared him. He died in Philadelphia, January 7, 1814, aged sixty-three years.

Levi Allen joined in the expedition to capture Ticonderoga, became Tory, and was complained of by his brother Ethan as follows:

BENNINGTON COUNTY, *ss.:*

ARLINGTON, 9 January, 1779.

To the Hon. the Court of Confiscation, comes Col. Ethan Allen, in the name of the freemen of the state, and complaint makes that Levi Allen, late of Salisbury in Connecticut, is of Tory principles and holds in fee sundry tracts and parcels of land in this State. The said Levi, has been detected in endeavoring to supply the enemy on Long Island; and in attempting to circulate counterfeit continental money, and is guilty of holding treasonable correspondence with the enemy under cover of doing favors to me when a prisoner at New York and Long Island; and in talking and using influence in favor of the enemy, associating with inimical persons to this country, and with them monopolizing the necessaries of life; in endeavoring to lessen the credit of the continental currency, and in particular hath exerted himself in the most fallacious manner to injure the property and character of some of the most zealous friends to the independence of the U. S. and of this State likewise: all which inimical conduct is against the peace and dignity of the freemen of this State. I therefore pray the Hon. Court to take the matter under their consideration and make confiscation of the estate of said Levi before mentioned, according to the laws and customs of this State, in such case made and provided.

ETHAN ALLEN.

Levi died while in jail, for debt, at Burlington, Vermont, in 1801.

Zimri lived and died in Sheffield.

Lydia married a Mr. Finch, and lived and died in Goshen, Connecticut.

Lucy married a Dr. Beebee, and lived and died in Sheffield.

CHAPTER II.

THE life of Allen may be divided into four
periods: the first thirty-one years before he
came to Vermont (1738–1769), the six years in
Vermont before his captivity (1769–1775), the
two years and eight months of captivity (1775–
1778), and the eleven years in Vermont after
his captivity (1778–1789).

When he was two years old the family moved
into Cornwall. There his brothers and sisters
were born, there his father died, there Ethan
lived until he was twenty-four years old.
When seventeen he was fitting for college with
the Rev. Mr. Lee, of Salisbury. His father's
death put an end to his studies. This was in
1755, when the French and Indian war was
raging along Lakes George and Champlain,
a war which lasted until Allen's twenty-third
year. Some of the early settlers of Vermont,
Samuel Robinson, Joseph Bowker, and others,

took part in this war. Not so Allen. There is no intimation that he hungered for a soldier's life in his youth. His usual means of earning a livelihood for himself and his widowed mother's family is supposed to have been agriculture.

William Cothrens, in his "History of Ancient Woodbury," tells us that in January, 1762, Allen, with three others, entered into the iron business in Salisbury, Connecticut, and built a furnace. In June of that year he returned to Roxbury, and married Mary Brownson, a maiden five years older than himself. The marriage fee was four shillings, or sixty-seven cents. By this wife he had five children: one son, who died at the age of eleven, while Ethan was a captive, and four daughters. Two died unmarried; one married Eleazer W. Keyes, of Burlington; the other married the Hon. Samuel Hitchcock, of Burlington, and was the mother of General Ethan Allen Hitchcock, U. S. A.

Allen resided with his family first at Salisbury and afterward at Sheffield, the southwest corner town of Massachusetts. For six miles the boundary line of the two states is the boundary line of the two towns. In these

towns the families of Ethan Allen and his
brothers and sisters lived many years. Two
years after moving to Salisbury he bought
two and a half acres, or one-sixteenth part
of a tract of land on Mine Hill, an eleva-
tion of 350 feet in Roxbury, containing, it is
said, the most remarkable deposit of spathic
iron ore in the United States. Immense sums
of money were expended in vain attempts to
work it as a silver mine. Two years after
Allen began his Vermont life he still owned
land in Judea Society, a part of the present
town of Washington. The details and financial results of these business undertakings are
not furnished us. They indicate enterprise, if
nothing more. Carrying on a farm, casting
iron ware, and working a mine, not military
affairs, seem to have been the avenues wherein
Allen developed his executive ability during
his early manhood.

What were his educational facilities, his social privileges, and his religious views during
this formative period of his life? Ira Allen,
in 1795, writes to Dr. S. Williams, the early
historian of Vermont, that when his father,
Joseph Allen, died, his brother Ethan was preparing for college, and that the death of his

father obliged Ethan to discontinue his clas-
sical studies. Mr. Jehial Johns, of Hunting-
ton, told the Rev. Zadock Thompson that he
knew Ethan Allen in Connecticut, and. was
very certain that Allen spent some time studying with the Rev. Mr. Lee, of Salisbury, with
the view of fitting himself for college. The
widow of Judge Samuel Hitchcock, of Burlington, told Mr. Thompson that Ethan's attend-
ance at school did not exceed three months.
Ira Allen writes General Haldimand in July,
1781, that his brother Ethan has resigned his
Brigadier-Generalship in the Vermont militia,
and "returned to his old studies, philosophy."
To what period in Ethan's life does the phrase
"old studies" refer? It could not be his life
after the captivity, during his five years' col-
lisions with the Yorkers, but the period we
are now considering. Heman Allen's widow,
when Mrs. Wadhams, told Zadock Thompson
that one summer when he was residing in her
house he passed almost all the time in writing.
She did not know what was the subject of his
study, but on one occasion she called him to
dinner, and he said he was very sorry she had
called him so soon, for he had "got clear up
into the upper regions." Allen himself says:

In my youth I was much disposed to contemplation, and at my commencement in manhood I committed to manuscript such sentiments or arguments as appeared most consonant to reason, lest through the debility of memory, my improvement should have been less gradual. This method of scribbling I practised for many years, from which I experienced great advantages in the progression of learning and knowledge; the more so as I was deficient in education and had to acquire the knowledge of grammar and language, as well as the art of reasoning, principally from a studious application to it; which after all, I am sensible, lays me under disadvantages, particularly in matters of composition; however, to remedy this defect I have substituted the most unwearied pains. . . . Ever since I arrived at the state of manhood and acquainted myself with the general history of mankind, I have felt a sincere passion for liberty. The history of nations doomed to perpetual slavery in consequence of yielding up to tyrants their natural-born liberties, I read with a sort of philosophical horror.

In Allen's youth great revivals were inaugurated, organized, and continued mainly by the preaching of Whitefield, who roused and electrified audiences of several thousands, as men have rarely been moved since the days of Peter the Hermit. Even Franklin, Bolingbroke, and Chesterfield were fascinated by him.

As for Allen, baptized in his infancy, in the days when no Sabbath-school blessed the race, when the Westminster Catechism and Watts' Hymns were in use throughout New England (Isaac Watts died when Allen was eleven years old), living in and near northwest Connecticut in as democratic and religious community as the world had ever seen, reading none of the books of the Deists, he was fond of discussion and delighted in writing out his arguments. Having been brought up an Armenian Christian, in contradistinction to a Calvinistic Christian, his views in early manhood began to change. One picture of this gradual evolution he gives us in the following description:

The doctrine of imputation according to the Christian scheme consists of two parts. First, of imputation of the apostasy of Adam and Eve to their posterity, commonly called original sin; and secondly, of the imputation of the merits or righteousness of Christ, who in Scripture is called the second Adam to mankind or to the elect. This is a concise definition of the doctrine, and which will undoubtedly be admitted to be a just one by every denomination of men who are acquainted with Christianity, whether they adhere to it or not.

I therefore proceed to illustrate and explain the doctrine by transcribing a short but very perti-

nent conversation which in the early days of my
manhood I had with a Calvinistic divine; but
previously remark that I was educated in what
are commonly called the Armenian principles;
and among other tenets to reject the doctrine of
original sin; this was the point at issue between
the clergyman and me.   In my turn I opposed
the doctrine of original sin with philosophical
reasonings, and as I thought had confuted the
doctrine.   The Reverend gentleman heard me
through patiently: and with candor replied:

"Your metaphysical reasonings are not to the
purpose, inasmuch as you are a Christian and hope
and expect to be saved by the imputed righteousness of Christ to you; for you may as well be imputedly sinful as imputedly righteous.   Nay," said
he, "if you hold to the doctrine of satisfaction and
atonement by Christ, by so doing you presuppose
the doctrine of apostasy or original sin to be in
fact true;" for, said he, "if mankind were not in a
ruined and condemned state by nature, there could
have been no need of a Redeemer; but each individual of them would have been accountable to his
Creator and Judge, upon the basis of his own
moral agency.   Further observing that upon philosophical principles it was difficult to account for
the doctrine of original sin, or of original righteousness; yet as they were plain, fundamental doc-
trines of the Christian faith we ought to assent to
the truth of them; and that from the divine authority of revelation.   Notwithstanding," said he,

"if you will give me a philosophical explanation of origial imputed righteousness, which you profess to believe and expect salvation by, then I will return you a philosophical explanation of original sin; for it is plain," said he, "that your objections lie with equal weight against original imputed righteousness, as against original imputed sin."

Upon which I had the candor to acknowledge to the worthy ecclesiastic, that upon the Christian plan I perceived the argument had clearly terminated against me. For at that time I dared not to distrust the infallibility of revelation; much more to dispute it. However, this conversation was uppermost in my mind for several months after; and after many painful searches and researches after the truth, respecting the doctrine of imputation, resolved at all events to abide the decision of rational argument in the premises; and on a full examination of both parts of the doctrine, rejected the whole; for on a fair scrutiny, I found that I must concede to it entirely or not at all; or else believe inconsistently as the clergyman had argued.

He relates also a change from his juvenile views of biblical history:

When I was a boy, by one means or other, I had conceived a very bad opinion of Pharaoh; he seemed to me to be a cruel, despotic prince; he would not give the Israelites straw, but nevertheless, demanded of them the full tale of brick; for a time he opposed God Almighty; but was at last luckily drowned in the Red Sea; at which event, with other good Christians, I rejoiced, and even exulted at the overthrow of the base and wicked tyrant. But after a few years of maturity and examination of the history of that monarch given by Moses, with the before recited remarks of the apostle, I conceived a more favorable opinion of him; inasmuch as we are told that God raised him up and hardened his heart, and predestinated his reign, his wickedness, and his overthrow.

In 1782 he says:

In the circle of my acquaintance (which has not been small), I have generally been denominated a Deist, the reality of which I never disputed; being conscious I am no Christian, except mere infant baptism makes me one; and as to being a Deist, I know not, strictly speaking, whether I am one or not, for I have never read their writings.

We are told that Allen in his early life was very intimate with Dr. Thomas Young, the man who supplied the state with its name, "Vermont," in April, 1777, and who so strongly encouraged it to assert its independence. One of the most noted characteristics of Ethan, his fondness for the society of able men, is illustrated in his association with Young.

Dr. Young, who was a distinguished citizen of

Philadelphia, was on most of the Whig committees in Boston, before the Revolution, with
James Otis, Samuel Adams, Joseph Warren,
and others. He and Adams addressed the
great public meeting on the day "when Boston
harbor was black with unexpected tea." He
was a neighbor of Allen, living in the Oblong,
in Dutchess County, while Allen lived in Salisbury. Afterward he lived in Albany, and died
in Philadelphia in the third year of Allen's
captivity. He was influential in causing Vermont to adopt the constitution of Pennsylvania.

The Oblong, Salisbury and vicinity, abound-
ed in free thinkers. Young and Allen opposed
President Edwards' famous theological tenets,
the latter spending much time in Young's
house, and it was generally understood that they
were preparing for publication a book in support
of sceptical principles; the two agreeing that
the one that outlived the other should publish
it. Allen, on going to Vermont, left his manuscripts with Young, and on his release from
captivity after Young's death obtained from
the latter's family, who had gone back to
Dutchess County, both his own and Young's
manuscripts, and these were the originals of
his "Oracles of Reason."

CHAPTER III.

ALLEN came to Vermont, probably, in 1769,
a year memorable for the founding of Dart-
mouth College and for the birth of four of
earth's renowned men: two soldiers, Welling-
ton and Napoleon; two scholars, Cuvier and
Humboldt.

In the early history of Vermont, one of its
prominent judges speculated extensively in
Green Mountain wild lands. The aggregate
result of these speculations was disastrous.
Attending a session of the legislature, the
judge was called upon by a committee for his
advice in reference to suitable penalties for
some crime. He replied, advising for the first
offence a fine; for the second, imprisonment;
and if the criminal should prove such a hardened offender, such a veteran in vice as to be
guilty the third time, he recommended that
the scoundrel should be compelled to receive

a deed of a mile square of wild Vermont lands.
Speculation in wild lands is a feature of pioneer
society. Vermont was once the agricultural
Eldorado of New England. Emigration first
rolled northward. Since that time a certain
star, erroneously supposed to belong to Bishop
Berkeley, has been travelling westward.

In 1749 Benning Wentworth, Governor of
New Hampshire, issued a patent of a township,
six miles square, near the northwest angle of
Massachusetts and corresponding with its line
northward, and in this township of Bennington the Allens bought lands and made their
home. This grant caused a remonstrance from
the governor and council of New York. Similar remonstrances had been made in the cases
of Connecticut and Massachusetts, each of
whom claimed that their territory extended
to the Connecticut River. But that question
had been settled in the former cases between
New York and New England by agreeing upon
a line from the southwest corner of Connecticut
northerly to Lake Champlain as the boundary
between the provinces. Wentworth urged in
justification of his course that the boundary line
was well known, and that New Hampshire had
the same right as the other colonies of New

England, and he persevered in his own course. In 1754 fourteen new townships had been granted, when the French war broke out and the settlers were deterred from occupying their lands by the incursions of the French and Indians on the frontier and the uncertainty of the termination of the contest; but when Canada was reduced by the English and peace concluded, there was a new rush for the possession of the fertile lands by the hardy and adventurous sons of the old New England colonies. In four years Governor Wentworth granted one hundred and thirty-eight townships, and the territory included was called the New Hampshire Grants. Then began in bitter earnest the long controversy between New York and New Hampshire for the ownership of all the territory now known as Vermont.

In order to make clear the circumstances of the time when Ethan Allen came to the front, it is necessary to explain something of the origin of the strife. The New York claim was founded on a charter given by Charles II. to his brother, the Duke of York, in 1664, for the country lying between the Connecticut and Delaware rivers. But that charter had long been considered as practically a nullity, for when the Duke of York succeeded to the throne of England, it all became public property subject to the king's divisions; and there are strong reasons for believing that the mention of the Connecticut was merely a formality, not intended as a definite boundary, and that the design was to take in the whole of the New Netherlands. The geography of the country was little known, and the wording of the charter was ambiguous and vague. Allen at once espoused the cause of the settlers. But for him the State of Vermont would probably have never existed. But for Allen, Albany, not Montpelier, might have been the capital of Vermont. Allen's most illustrious achievement for the benefit of the nation was the capture of Ticonderoga. His great work for Vermont was successful resistance to the Yorkers.

Before entering upon this period of litigation, one of the stories of Allen, illustrating his honesty, may fitly find a place. Having given a note which he was unable to pay when it became due, he was sued. Allen employed a lawyer to attend to his case and postpone payment. But the lawyer could not

3

prevent the rendering a judgment against Allen at the first term of court, unless he filed a plea alleging some real or fictitious ground of defence. Accordingly, quite innocently he put in the usual plea denying that Allen signed the note. The effect of this was to continue the case to the next term of court, exactly what Allen wanted; but Allen was present and was indignant that he should be made to appear to sanction a falsehood. He rose in court and vehemently denounced his lawyer, telling him that he did not employ him to tell a lie; he did sign that note; he wanted to pay it; he only wanted time!

It was in June, 1770, that Allen first became prominent in Vermont public affairs. Then it was that the lawsuits brought by Yorkers for Vermont lands were tried before the Supreme Court at Albany. Robert R. Livingston was the presiding judge; Kempe and Duane, attorneys for plaintiffs; Silvester, of Albany, and Jared Ingersoll, of New Haven, attorneys for defendants. Ethan Allen was active in preparing the defence. But of what avail was defence when the court was virtually an adverse party to the suit? Not only did Duane claim 50,000 acres of

Vermont lands, but, to the disgrace of English jurisprudence, Livingston, the presiding judge, was interested directly or indirectly in 30,000 acres. The farce was soon played out; the court refused to hear the New Hampshire charter read; one trial was sufficient; the plaintiffs won all the cases. Duane and others called on Allen and reminded him that "might makes right," advising him to go home and counsel compromise. Allen observed: "The gods of the valleys are not the gods of the hills!" Duane asked for an explanation, and Allen replied: "If you will come to Bennington the meaning shall be made clear to you."

Allen went home and no compromise was thought of. The great seal of New Hampshire being disregarded, the "Beech Seal" was invented as a substitute. A military organization was formed with several companies, Seth Warner, Remember Baker, and others as captains, and Ethan Allen as colonel.

In July, 1771, on the farm of James Breakenridge, in Bennington, the State of Vermont was born. Ten Eyck, the sheriff, with 300 men, including mayor, aldermen, lawyers, and others, issued forth from Albany, as did De Soto to capture Florida, as Don Quixote essayed to conquer the windmills. Breakenridge's family were wisely absent. In his house were eighteen armed men provided with a red flag to run up the chimney as a signal for aid. The house was barricaded and provided with loop-holes. On the woody ridge north were 100 armed men, their heads and the muzzles of their guns barely visible amid the foliage. To the southeast, in plain sight, was a smaller body of men within gunshot of the house. Six or seven guarded the bridge half a mile to the west. Mayor Cuyler and a few others were allowed to cross the bridge and a parley ensued. The mayor returned to the bridge, and in half an hour the sheriff was notified that possession would be kept at all hazards. He ordered the posse to advance, and a small portion reluctantly complied. Another parley followed, while lawyer Yates expounded New York law and the Vermonters justified their position. The sheriff seized an axe, and going toward the door, threatened to break it open. In an instant an array of guns was aimed at him; he stopped, retired to the bridge, and ordered the posse to advance five miles into Bennington. But the Yorkers stampeded for home, and the bubble burst. The "star that never sets" had begun to glimmer upon the horizon.

In the winter of 1771–72 Governor Tryon, of New York, issued proclamations heavy with ponderous logic and shotted with offers of money for the arrest of Allen and others. To the arguments Allen replied through a newspaper, the Connecticut *Courant*, of Hartford. To the premium for his arrest he returned a Roland for an Oliver in the following placard:

£25 Reward.—Whereas James Duane and John Kempe, of New York, have by their menaces and threats greatly disturbed the public peace and repose of the honest peasants of Bennington and the settlements to the northward, which are now and ever have been in the peace of God and the King, and are patriotic and liege subjects of Geo. the 3d. Any person that will apprehend those common disturbers, viz: James Duane and John Kempe, and bring them to Landlord Fay's, at Bennington, shall have £15 reward for James Duane and £10 reward for John Kempe, paid by

Dated Poultney,
  Feb. 5, 1772.

ETHAN ALLEN.
REMEMBER BAKER.
ROBERT COCHRAN.

Duane and Kempe were prominent lawyers of New York, and also prominent as advocates of New York's claim to Vermont lands. Duane was the son-in-law of Robert Livingston and Kempe was attorney-general. The idea of their being kidnapped for exhibition at a log tavern in the wilderness was slightly grotesque. But this did not satisfy Allen. He would fain visit the enemy in one of his strongholds.

Albany was emphatically a Dutch city, for it was two centuries old before it had 10,000 inhabitants. In 1772 it might have had half that number. While the country was flooded with proclamations for his arrest, Allen rode alone into the city. Slowly passing through the streets to the principal hotel he dismounted, entered the bar-room, and called for a bowl of punch. The news circulated; the Dutch rallied; the crowd centred at the hotel; the officers of the court, the valiant sheriff, Ten Eyck, and the attorney-general were present. Allen raised the punch-bowl, bowed courteously to the crowd, swallowed the beverage, returned to the street, remounted his horse, rose in his stirrups and shouted "Hurrah for the Green Mountains!" and then leisurely rode away unharmed and unmolested. The incident illustrates Allen's shrewd courage, and sustains Governor Hall's theory that the people of New York sympathized more with the Green Mountain Boys than with their own land-gambling officers.

At the Green Mountain tavern in Bennington was a sign-post, with a sign twenty-five feet from the ground. Over the sign was the stuffed skin of a catamount with large teeth grinning toward New York. A Dutchman of Arlington who had been active against the Green Mountain Boys was punished by being tied in an arm-chair, hoisted to this sign, and there suspended for two hours, to the amusement of the juvenile population and the quiet gratification of their seniors.

CHAPTER IV.

DURING the six years preceding the Revolution, Allen was the most prominent leader of the Green Mountain Boys in all matters of peace, and also in political writing. When the Manchester Convention, October 21, 1772, sent James Breakenridge, of Bennington, and Jehiel Hawley, of Arlington, as delegates to England, perhaps Allen could not be spared, for if any New York document needed answering Allen answered it; if any handbill, proclamation or counter-statement, or political or legal argument was to be written, Allen wrote it; if New England was to be informed of the Yorkers' rascalities, Allen sent the information to the Connecticut *Courant* and Portsmouth *Gazette*, Vermont having no newspaper. Rarely was force or threat used or a rough joke played on a Yorker, but Allen was first in the

32

fray. In Bennington County Allen with others told a Yorker that they had "that morning resolved to offer a burnt sacrifice to the gods of the woods in burning the logs of his house." They did burn the logs and the rafters, and told him to go and complain to his "scoundrel governor."

Of all the towns of Western Vermont, Clarendon had been most noted for its Tories and its Yorkers. Settled as early as 1768, its settlers founded their claims to land titles on grants from three different powers: Colonel Lydius, New York, and New Hampshire. The New York patent of Socialborough, covering Rutland and Pittsford substantially, was dated April 3, 1771, and issued by Governor Dunmore. The New York patent of Durham, dated January 7, 1772, issued by Governor Tryon, covered Clarendon. Both were in direct violation of the royal order in council, July, 1767, and therefore illegal and void. The new county of Charlotte, created March 12, 1772, extended from Canada into Arlington and Sunderland and west of Lake George and Lake Champlain. Benjamin Spencer, of Durham, was a justice and judge of the new county; Jacob Marsh, of Socialborough, a justice; and Simeon Jenny, who lived near Chippenhook, coroner. These three officers were zealous New York partisans. The Green Mountain Boys in council passed resolutions to the effect that no citizen should do any official act under New York authority; that all persons holding Vermont lands should hold them under New Hampshire laws, and if necessary force should be used to enforce these resolves.

In the early part of the fall of 1773, a large force of Green Mountain Boys, under Ethan Allen and other leaders, visited Clarendon and requested the Yorkers to comply with these resolutions, informing them if this were not done within a reasonable time the persons of the Durhamites would suffer. Justice Spencer absconded. No violence was used except on one poor innocent dog of the name of Tryon, and Governor Tryon was so odious that the dog was cut in pieces without benefit of clergy. This display of force and the threats that were very freely used, it was hoped, would be enough to secure submission, but the justices still issued writs against the New Hampshire settlers; other New York officials acted, and all were loud in advocating the New York title.

A second visit to Durham was made. Saturday, November 20, at 11 P.M., Ethan Allen, Remember Baker, and twenty to thirty others surrounded Spencer's house, took him prisoner, and carried him two miles to the house of one Green, where he was kept under a guard of four men until Monday morning, and then taken "to the house of Joseph Smith, of Durham, innkeeper." He was asked where he preferred to be tried; he replied that he was not guilty of any crime, but if he must be tried, he should choose his own door as the place of trial. The Green Mountain Boys had now increased in number to about one hundred and thirty, armed with guns, cutlasses, and other weapons. The people of Clarendon, Rutland, and Pittsford hearing of the trial, gathered to witness the proceedings. A rural lawsuit still has a wonderful fascination for a rural populace. Allen addressed the crowd, telling them that he, with Remember Baker, Seth Warner, and Robert Cochran, had been appointed to inspect and set things in order; that "Durham had become a hornets' nest" which must be broken up. A "judgment seat" was erected; Allen, Warner, Baker, and Cochran took seats thereon as judges, and Spencer was ordered to stand before this tribunal, take off his hat, and listen to the accusations. Allen accused him of joining with New York land jobbers against New Hampshire grantees and issuing a warrant as a justice. Warner accused him of accepting a New York commission as a magistrate, of acting under it, of writing a letter hostile to New Hampshire, of selling land bought of a New York grantee, and of trying to induce people to submit to New York. He was found guilty, his house declared a nuisance, and the sentence was pronounced that his house be burnt, and that he promise not to act again as a New York justice. Spencer declared that if his house were burned, his store of dry-goods and all his property would be destroyed and his wife and children would be great sufferers. Thereupon the sentence was reconsidered. Warner suggested that his house be not destroyed, but that the roof be taken off and put on again, provided Spencer should acknowledge that it was put on under a New Hampshire title and should purchase a New Hampshire title. The judges so decided. Spencer promised compliance, and "with great shouting" the roof was taken off and replaced, and this pioneer dry-goods store of 1773 was preserved.

At another time twenty or thirty of Allen's party visit the house of Coroner Jenny. The house was deserted; Jenny had fled, and they burned the house to the ground. The other Durhamites were visited and threatened, and they agreed to purchase New Hampshire titles. Some of the party returning from Clarendon met Jacob Marsh in Arlington, on his way from New York to Rutland. They seized him and put him on trial. Warner and Baker were the accusers. Baker wished to apply the "beech seal," but the judges declined. Warner read the sentence that he should encourage New Hampshire settlers, discourage New York settlers, and not act as a New York justice, "upon pain of having his house burnt and reduced to ashes and his person punished at their pleasure." He was then dismissed with the following certificate:

Arlington, Nov. 25, A.D. 1773. These may sertify that Jacob Marsh haith been examined, and had a fare trial, so that our mob shall not meadel farther with him as long as he behaves.

Sertified by us as his judges, to wit,

NATHANIEL SPENCER,
SAML. TUBS,
PHILIP PERRY.

On reaching home, Marsh found that the roof of his house had been publicly taken off by the Green Mountain Boys.

Spencer in his letter to Duane, April 11, 1772, wrote: "One Ethan Allen hath brought from Connecticut twelve or fifteen of the most blackguard fellows he can get, double-armed, in order to protect him." This same Spencer, after acting as a Whig and one of the Council of Safety, deserted to Burgoyne in 1777, and died a few weeks after at Ticonderoga.

Benjamin Hough, of Clarendon, was a troublesome New York justice. His neighbors seized him and carried him thirty miles south in a sleigh. After three days, January 30, 1775, he was tried in Sunderland before Allen and others. His punishment was two hundred lashes on the naked back while he was tied to a tree. Allen and Warner signed a written certificate as a burlesque passport for Hough to New York, "he behaving as becometh."

At this time the following open letters from the Green Mountain Boys were published:

An epistle to the inhabitants of Clarendon: From Mr. Francis Madison of your town, I understand Oliver Colvin of your town has acted the infamous part by locating part of the farm of said Madison. This sort of trick I was partly apprised of, when I wrote the late letter to Messrs. Spencer and Marsh. I abhor to put a staff into the hands of Colvin or any other rascal to defraud your letter. The Hampshire title must, nay shall, be had for such settlers as are in quest of it, at a reasonable rate, nor shall any villain by a sudden purchase impose on the old settlers. I advise said Colvin to be flogged for the abuse aforesaid, unless he immediately retracts and reforms, and if there be further difficulties among you, I advise that you employ Capt. Warner as an arbitrator in your affairs. I am certain he will do all parties justice. Such candor you need in your present situation, for I assure you, it is not the design of our mobs to betray you into the hands of villainous purchasers. None but blockheads would purchase your farms, and they must be treated as such. If this letter does not settle this dispute, you had better hire Captain Warner to come simply and assist you in the settlement of your affairs. My business is such that I cannot attend to your matters in person, but desire you would inform me, by writing or otherwise relative thereto. Captain Baker joins with the foregoing, and does me the honor to subscribe his name with me. We are, gentlemen, your friends to serve.

ETHAN ALLEN,
REMEMBER BAKER.

To Mr. Benjamin Spencer and Mr. Amos Marsh, and the people of Clarendon in general:

GENTLEMEN:—On my return from what you called the mob, I was concerned for your welfare, fearing that the force of our arms would urge you to purchase the New Hampshire title at an unreasonable rate, tho' at the same time I know not but after the force is withdrawn, you will want a third army. However, on proviso, you incline to purchase the title aforesaid, it is my opinion, that you in justice ought to have it at a reasonable rate, as new lands were valued at the time you purchased them. This, with sundry other arguments in your behalf, I laid before Captain Jehiel Hawley and other respectable gentlemen of that place (Arlington) and by their advice and concurrence, I write you this friendly epistle unto which they subscribe their names with me, that we are disposed to assist you in purchasing reasonably as aforesaid; and on condition Colonel Willard, or any other person demand an exorbitant price for your lands we scorn it, and will assist you in mobbing such avaricious persons, for we mean to use force against oppression, and that only. Be it in New York, Willard, or any person, it is injurious to the rights of the district.

From yours to serve. ETHAN ALLEN,
JEHIEL HAWLEY,
DANIEL CASTLE,
GIDEON HAWLEY,
REUBEN HAWLEY,
ABEL HAWLEY.

The convention had decreed that no officer from New York should attempt to take any person out of its territory, on penalty of a severe punishment, and it forbade any surveyor to run lines through the lands or inspect them with that purpose. This edict enlarged the powers of the military commanders, and it was their duty to search out such offenders. The Committees of Safety which were chosen were entrusted with powers for regulating local affairs, and the conventions of delegates representing the people, which assembled from time to time, adopted measures tending to harmony and concentration of effort.

May 19, 1772 (the year in which occurred Poland's first dismemberment), Governor Tryon wrote to Bennington and vicinity, inviting the citizens to send delegates to him and explain the causes of their opposition to New York rule. Could anything be fairer or more politic and wise? He promised safety to any and all sent, except four of their leaders, Allen, Warner, Cochran, and Sevil, and suggested sending their pastor, J. Dewey, and Mr. Fay. Dewey answered on June 5:

We, his Majesty's leal and loyal subjects of the Province of New York. . . . First, we hold

4

fee of our land by grants of George II., and George III., the lands reputed then in New Hampshire. Since 1764, New York has granted the same land as though the fee of the land and property was altered with jurisdiction, which we suppose was not. . . . Suits of law for our lands rejecting our proof of title, refusing time to get our evidence are the grounds of our discontent. . . . Breaking houses for possession of them, and their owners, firing on these people and wounding innocent women and children. . . . We must closely adhere to the maintaining our property with a due submission to Your Excellency's jurisdiction. . . . We pray and beseech Your Excellency would assist to quiet us in our possessions, till his Majesty in his royal wisdom shall be graciously pleased to settle the controversy.

Allen, not being allowed to go to New York, wrote to Tryon in conjunction with Warner, Baker, and Cochran, stating the case as follows:

No consideration whatever, shall induce us to remit in the least of our loyalty and gratitude to our most Gracious Sovereign, and reasonably to you; yet no tyranny shall deter us from asserting and vindicating our rights and privileges as Englishmen. We expect an answer to our humble petition, delivered you soon after you became Governor, but in vain. We assent to your jurisdiction, because it is the King's will, and always

have, except where perverse use would deprive us
of our property and country. We desire and petition to be reannexed to New Hampshire. That is
not the principal cause we object to, but we think
change made by fraud, unconstitutional exercise of
it. The New York patentees got judgments, took
out writs, and actually dispossessed several by
order of law, of their houses and farms and necessaries. These families spent their fortunes in bring-
ing wilderness into fruitful fields, gardens and
orchards. Over fifteen hundred families ejected,
if five and one-quarter persons are allowed to
each family. . . . The writs of ejectment come
thicker and faster. . . . Nobody can be supposed under law if law does not protect. . . .
Since our misfortune of being annexed to New
York, law is a tool to cheat us. . . . Fatigued
in settling a wilderness country. . . . As our
cause is before the King, we do not expect you to
determine it. . . . If we don't oppose Sheriff,
he takes our houses and farms. If we do, we are
indicted rioters. If our friends help us, they are
indicted rioters. As to refugees, self-preservation
necessitated our treating some of them roughly.
Ebenezer Cowle and Jonathan Wheat, of Shaftsbury, fled to New York, because of their own
guilt, they not being hurt nor threatened. John
Munro, Esq., and ruffians, assaulting Baker at daybreak, March 22, was a notorious riot, cutting,
wounding and maiming Mr. Baker, his wife and
children. As Baker is alive he has no cause of
complaint. Later he (Munro) assaulted Warner

who, with a dull cutlass, struck him on the head to the ground.   As laws are made by our enemies, we could not bring Munro to justice otherwise than by mimicing him, and treating him as he did Baker, and so forth.   Bliss Willoughby, feigning business, went to Baker's house and reported to Munro, thus instigating and planning the attack. . . . The alteration of jurisdiction in 1764 could not affect private property. . . . The transferring or alienation of property is a sacred prerogative of the true owner.   Kings and Governors cannot intermeddle therewith. . . . We have a petition lying before his Majesty and Council for redress of our grievances for several years past. In Moore's time, the King forbid New York to patent any lands before granted by New Hampshire.   This a supercedeas of Common Law. King notifying New York he takes cognizance and will settle and forbids New York to meddle: common sense teaches a common law, judgment after that, if it prevailed, would be subversive of royal authority.   So all officers coming to dispossess are violaters of law.   Right and wrong are externally the same.   We are not opposing you and your Government, but a party chiefly attorneys.   We hear you applied to assembly for armed force to subdue us in vain.   We choose Captain Stephen Fay and Mr. Jonas Fay, to treat with you in person.   We entreat your aid to quiet us in our farms till the King decides it.*

* This letter, like others, is given verbatim, despite some evident errors of phraseology.

The embassy was successful. The council advised that all legal processes against Vermont should cease. If Bennington was happy in May over the invitation, Bennington was jubilant in August over the kindly advice. The air rang with shouts; the health of governor and council was drunk and cannon and small-arms were heard everywhere. No part of New York colony was happier or more devotedly British. Two years had passed since the New York Supreme Court had adjudged all the Vermont legal documents null and void: one year had passed since New York had sent a sheriff and posse with hundreds of citizens to force Vermont farmers from their farms, but both of these affairs occurred under Governor Clinton. Now perhaps, the Vermonters thought, the new governor was going to act fairly: there would be no more fights; no more watching and guarding against midnight attacks; no more need of fire-arms; and wives and babes would be safe. There would be no more kidnapping of Green Mountain Boys and hurrying them away to Albany jail; no more foreign surveying of the lands they tilled and loved.

CHAPTER V.

BUT "best laid schemes of mice and men gang aft agley." While these negotiations were pending, New Yorkers were quietly doing the necessary work for stealing more Vermont lands. Cockburn, the Scotch New York surveyor, was surveying land along Otter Creek. The Green Mountain Boys heard of it, rallied, and overtook him near Vergennes, and found Colonel Reid's Scotchmen enjoying mills and farms. For three years these foreigners had been there. In 1769, with no legal title, they had found, seized, and enjoyed the land, with a mill. Vermonters had then rallied and dispossessed these dispossessors, but a second raid of Reid's men redispossessed them. In the summer of 1772, Vermont, seizing Cockburn, turned out Reid's tenants, broke up mill-stones and threw them over the falls, razed houses, and burned crops.

46

The Scotch story is as follows: John Cameron made affidavit that he and some other families from Scotland arrived at New York in the latter part of June, and a few days afterward agreed with Lieutenant-Colonel Reid to settle as tenants on his lands on Otter Creek, in Charlotte County. Reid went with them to Otter Creek, some miles east from Crown Point, and was at considerable expense in transporting them, their wives, children, and baggage. The day after their arrival at Otter Creek they were viewing the land, where they saw a crop of Indian corn, wheat, and garden stuff, and a stack of hay and two New England men. Reid paid these two men $15 for their crops, the men agreeing to leave until the king's pleasure should be known. Reid made over these crops to his new tenants, gave them possession of the land in presence of two justices of the peace of Charlotte County, and bought some provisions and cows for his tenants. On or about the 11th of August, armed men from different parts of the country came and turned James Henderson and others out of their homes, burnt the houses to the ground, and for two days pastured fifty horses which they had brought with them in a field of corn which Reid had bought. They also burnt a large stack of hay, purchased by Reid. The next day the rioters, headed by their captains, Allen, Baker, and Warner, came to Cameron's house, destroyed the new grist-mill, built by Reid (Baker insisting upon it), broke the mill-stones in pieces and threw them down a precipice into the river. The rioters then turned out Cameron's wife and two small children, and burnt the house, having in the two days burnt five houses, two corn shades, and one stack of hay. When Cameron, much incensed, asked by what authority of law they committed such violences, Baker replied that they lived out of the bounds of law, and holding up his gun said that was his law. He further declared that they were resolved never to allow any persons claiming under New York to settle in that part of the province, but if Cameron would join them, they would give him lands for nothing. This offer Cameron rejected. While the rioters were destroying his house and mill on the Crown Point (west) side of Otter Creek, he heard six men ordered to go with arms and stand as sentinels on a rising ground toward Crown Point, to prevent any surprise from the troops in the garrison there.

Having destroyed Cameron's house and the mill, the rioters recrossed the river. Cameron reports that he saw among the rioters Joshua Hide, who had agreed in writing with Reid not to return, and had received payment for his crop. Hide was very active in advising the destruction of Cameron's house and the mill.

Cameron stayed about three weeks at Otter Creek, after the rioters dispersed, hoping to hear from Reid, and hoping also that New York would protect him and his fellow-settlers, but having no house, and being exposed to the night air, the fever and ague soon compelled him to retire. Some of his companions went before, the rest were to follow. What became of his wife and children he does not state. Cameron stayed one night at the house of a Mr. Irwin, on the east shore of the lake, five miles north of Crown Point. Irwin, an elderly man, holding a New Hampshire title, told Cameron that Reid had a narrow escape, for Baker with eight men had laid in wait for him a whole day, near the mouth of Otter Creek, determined to murder him, and the men in the boat with him, on their way back to Crown Point, so that none might remain to tell tales.

Fortunately Reid had left the day before. Irwin disapproved of such bloody intentions, and said if his land was confirmed to a Yorker, he would either buy the Yorker's title or move off.

James Henderson, settler under Colonel Reid, deposed that on Wednesday, August 11, he and three others of Colonel Reid's settlers were at work at their hay in the meadow, when twenty men, armed with guns, swords, and pistols, surprised them. They inquired if Henderson and his companions lived in the house some time before occupied by Joshua Hide. They replied no, the men who lived in that house were about their business. The rioters then told Henderson and his companions that they must go along with them (as they could not understand the women), and marched them prisoners, guarded before and behind like criminals, to the house, where they joined the rest of the mob, in number about one hundred or more, all armed as before, and who, as Henderson was told by the women, had let their horses loose in the corn and wheat that Reid had bought for his settlers. The mob desired the things to be taken out of the house, and then set the house on fire. Ethan

Allen, the ringleader or captain, then ordered part of his gang to go with Henderson to his own house (formerly built and occupied by Captain Gray) in order to prepare it for the same fate. Henderson and his wife earnestly requested the mob to spare their house for a few days, in order to save their effects and protect their children from the inclemency of the weather, until they could have an opportunity of removing themselves to some safe place; but Captain Allen, coming up from the fore-mentioned house, told them that his business required haste; for he and his gang were determined not to leave a house belonging to Colonel Reid standing. Then the mob set fire to and entirely consumed Henderson's house. Henderson took out his memorandum book and desired to know their ringleader's or captain's name. The captain answered: "Who gave you authority to ask for my name?" Henderson replied that as he took him to be the ringleader of the mob, and as he had in such a riotous and unlawful manner dispossessed him, he had a right to ask his name, that he might represent him to Colonel Reid, who had put him, Henderson, in peaceable possession of the premises as his just

property. Allen answered, he wished they
had caught Colonel Reid; they would have
whipped him severely; that his name was
Ethan Allen, captain of that mob, and that
his authority was his own arms, pointing to
his gun; that he and his companions were a
lawless mob, their law being mob law. Henderson replied that the law was made for lawless and riotous people, and that he must know
it was death by the law to ringleaders of
rioters and lawless mobs. Allen answered
that he had run these woods in the same manner these seven years past [this would carry
it back to the year 1766, when Zadoc Thompson says Allen's family was living in Sheffield]
and never was caught yet; and he told Henderson that if any of Colonel Reid's settlers
offered hereafter to build any house and keep
possession, the Green Mountain Boys, as they
call themselves, would burn their houses and
whip them into the bargain. The mob then
burnt the house formerly built and occupied
by Lewis Stewart, and remained that night
about Leonard's house. The next day, about
seven A.M., August 12, Henderson went to
Leonard's house. The mob were all drawn
up, consulting about destroying the mill.

Those who were in favor of it were ordered to follow Captain Allen. In the mean time Baker and his gang came to the opposite side of the river and fired their guns. They were brought over at once, and while they were taking some refreshment, Allen's party marched to the mill, but did not break up any part of it until Allen joined them. The two mobs having joined (by their own account one hundred and fifty in number), with axes, crow-bars, and handspikes tore the mill to pieces, broke the mill-stones and threw them into the creek. Baker came out of the mill with the bolt-cloth in his hands. With his sword he cut it in pieces and distributed it among the mob to wear in their hats like cockades, as trophies of the victory. Henderson told Baker he was about very disagreeable work. Baker replied it was so, but he had a commission for so doing, and showed Henderson where his thumb had been cut off, which he called his commission.

Angus McBean, settler under Colonel Reid, deposed that between seven and eight A.M., Thursday, August 12 last, he met a part of the New England mob about Leonard's house, sixty men or thereabouts, he supposed, armed with guns, swords, and pistols. One of them asked Angus if he were one of Colonel Reid's new settlers, and having been told he was, asked him what he intended to do. McBean replied he intended to build himself a house and keep possession of the land. He was then asked if he intended to keep possession for Colonel Reid. He replied yes, as long as he could. Soon after their chief leader, Allen, came and asked him if he was the man that said he would keep possession for Colonel Reid. McBean said yes. Allen then damned his soul, but he would have him, McBean, tied to a tree and skinned alive, if he ever attempted such a thing. Allen and several of the mob said, if they could but catch Colonel Reid, they would cut his head off. Joshua Hide, one of the persons of whom Colonel Reid bought the crop, advised the mob to tear down or burn the houses of Donald McIntosh and John Burdan, as they both had been assisting Colonel Reid. Soon after several guns were fired on the other side of the creek. Some of the mob said that was Captain Baker and his party coming to see the sport. Soon Baker and his party joined the mob, and all went to tear down the grist-mill. McBean thought

Baker was one of the first that entered the mill.

However strong our indignation at the New York usurpations, we cannot read of the violent ejectment of families without a feeling of repugnance to such a method. Turn to the vivid and romantic account of Colonel Reid's settlement in "The Tory's Daughter," and remember that in civil strife the innocent must often suffer. The Green Mountain Boys' immunity from the penalty of the law for their riotous acts shows not only their adroitness, but suggests half-heartedness in their pursuit. Laws not supported by public sentiment are rarely enforced.

John Munroe wrote to Duane during the Clarendon proceedings:

The rioters have a great many friends in the county of Albany, and particularly in the city of Albany, which encourages them in their wickedness, at the same time hold offices under the Government, and pretend to be much against them, but at heart I know them to be otherwise, for the rioters have often told me, that be it known to me, that they had more friends in Albany than I had, which I believe to be true.

Hugh Munro lived near the west line of

Shaftsbury. He took Surveyor Campbell to survey land in Rupert for him. He was seized by Cochran, who said he was a son of Robin Hood, and beaten. Ira Allen says Munro fainted from whipping by bush twigs. Munro had not a savory reputation with the Vermonters. After Tryon's offer of a reward for the arrest of Allen, Baker, and Cochran, he, with ten or twelve other men, had seized Baker, who lived ten or twelve miles from him, a mile east of Arlington. After a march of sixteen miles, they were met by ten Bennington men, who arrested Munro and Constable Stevens, the rest of the party fleeing. Later Warner and one man rode to Munro's and asked for Baker's gun. Munro refused, and seizing Warner's bridle ordered the constable to arrest Warner, who drew his cutlass and felled Munro to the ground. For this act of Warner's, Poultney voted him one hundred acres of land April 4, 1773.

In 1774 Allen published a pamphlet of over two hundred pages, in which he rehearsed many historical facts tending to show that previous to the royal order of 1764, New York had no claim to extend easterly to the Connecticut River. He portrayed in strong light the oppressive conduct of New York toward the settlers. This pamphlet also contained the answer of himself and of his associates to the Act of Outlawry of March, 1774. Another man was busy this year drawing up reports of the trouble in Vermont.

Crean Brush, the first Vermont lawyer, was a colonel, a native of Dublin. In 1762 he came to New York and became assistant secretary of the colony; in 1771–74 he practised law in Westminster, Vt. He claimed thousands of Vermont acres under New York titles, and became county clerk, surrogate, and provincial member of Congress. He was in Boston jail nineteen months for plundering Boston whigs, and finally escaped in his wife's dress. The British commander in New York told him his conduct merited more punishment. A Yorker, always fighting the Green Mountain Boys; a tory, always fighting the whigs; with fair culture and talent, he became a sot, and, at the age of fifty-three, in 1778, he blew his brains out, in New York City. He left a step-daughter who became the second wife of Ethan Allen.

On February 5, 1774, Brush reported to the New York Legislature resolutions to the effect

5

"that riotousness exists in part of Charlotte County and northeast Albany County, calling for redress; that a Bennington mob has terrorized officers, rescued debtors, assumed military command and judicial power, burned houses, beat citizens, expelled thousands, stopped the administration of justice; that anti-rioters are in danger in person and property and need protection. Wherefore the Governor is petitioned to offer fifty pounds reward for the apprehension and lodgment in Albany jail of Ethan Allen, Seth Warner, Remember Baker, Robert Cochran, Peleg Sunderland, Silvanus Brown, James Breakenridge, and John Smith, either or any of them." It was ordered that Brush and Colonel Ten Eyck report a bill for the suppression of riotous and disorderly proceedings. Captain Delaney and Mr. Walton were appointed to present the address and resolutions to the governor.

A committee met March 1, 1774, at Eliakim Weller's house in Manchester, adjourning to the third Wednesday at Captain Jehial Hawley's in Arlington. Nathan Clark was chairman of the committee and Jonas Clark clerk. The *New York Mercury*, No. 1,163, with the foregoing report in it, was produced and read.

Seven of the committee were chosen to examine it and prepare a report, which was adopted and ordered published in the public papers. They speak of their misfortune in being annexed to New York, and hope that the king will adopt the report of the Board of Trade, made December 3, 1772. In consequence, hundreds of settled families, many of them comparatively wealthy, resolved to defend the outlawed men. All were ready at a minute's warning. They resolved to act on the defensive only, and to encourage the execution of law in civil cases and in real criminal cases. They advised the General Assembly to wait for the king's decision. The committee declared that they were all loyal to their political father; but that as they bought of the first governor appointed by the king, on the faith of the crown, they will maintain those grants; that New York has acted contrary to the spirit of the good laws of Great Britain. This declaration was certified by the chairman and clerk, at Bennington, April 14, 1774.

It was in 1774 that a new plan was formed for escaping from the government of New York; a plan that startles us by its audacity and its comprehensiveness. This was to establish a new royal colony extending from the Connecticut to Lake Ontario and the St. Lawrence, from forty-five degrees of north latitude to Massachusetts and the Mohawk River. The plan was formed by Allen and other Vermonters. At that time Colonel Philip Skene, a retired British officer, was living at Whitehall on a large patent of land., To him the Vermonters communicated the project. Whitehall was to be the capital and Skene the governor of the projected colony. Skene, at his own expense, went to London, and was appointed governor of Ticonderoga and Crown Point, but the course of public events prevented the completion of this scheme.

CHAPTER VI.

ON March 29, 1775, John Brown, a Massachusetts lawyer, wrote from Montreal to Boston:

The people on the New Hampshire Grants have engaged to seize the fort at Ticonderoga as soon as possible, should hostilities be committed by the king's troops.

The most minute account of the preparations to capture Ticonderoga is furnished by the diary for April, 1775, of Edward Mott, of Preston, Conn., a captain in Colonel S. H. Parson's regiment. He had been at the camp of the American army beleaguering Boston; took charge of the expedition to seize Ticonderoga; reported its success to Governor Trumbull at Hartford; was sent by Trumbull to Congress at Philadelphia with the news; resumed the command of his company at Ticonderoga in May; was with the Northern army during the campaign; was at the taking of Chambly and St. Johns; and became a major in Colonel Gray's regiment next year.

PRESTON, Friday, April 28, 1775.

Set out for Hartford, where I arrived the same day. Saw Christopher Leffingwell, who inquired of me about the situation of the people at Boston. When I had given him an account, he asked me how they could be relieved and where I thought we could get artillery and stores. I told him I knew not unless we went and took possession of Ticonderoga and Crown Point, which I thought might be done by surprise with a small number of men. Mr. Leffingwell left me and in a short time came to me again, and brought with him Samuel H. Parsons and Silas Deane, Esqrs. When he asked me if I would undertake in such an expedition as we had talked of before, I told him I would. They told me they wished I had been there one day sooner; that they had been on such a plan; and that they had sent off Messrs. Noah Phelps and Bernard Romans, whom they had supplied with £300 in cash from the treasury, and ordered them to draw for more if they should need; that said Phelps and Romans had gone by the way of Salisbury, where they would make a stop. They expected a small number of men would join them, and if I would go after them they would give me an order or letter to them to join with them and to have my voice with them in conducting the affair and in laying out the money; and also that I might take five or six men with me. On which I took with me Mr. Jeremiah Halsey, Mr. Epaphras Bull, Mr. Wm. Nichols, Mr. Elijah Babcock, and John Bigelow joined me; and Saturday, the 29th of April, in the afternoon, we set out on said expedition. Mr. Babcock tired his horse. We got another horse of Esq. Humphrey in Norfolk, and that day arrived at Salisbury; tarried all night, and the next day, having augmented our company to the number of sixteen in the whole, we concluded it was not best to add any more, as we meant to keep our business a secret and ride through the country unarmed till we came to the New Settlements on the Grants. We arrived at Mr. Dewey's in Sheffield, and there we sent off Mr. Jer. Halsey and Capt. John Stevens to go to Albany, in order to discover the temper of the people in that place, and to return and inform us as soon as possible.

That night (Monday the 1st of May) we arrived at Col. Easton's in Pittsfield, where we fell in company with John Brown, Esq., who had been at Canada and Ticonderoga about a month before; on which we concluded to make known our business to Col. Easton and said Brown and to take their advice on the same. I was advised by Messrs. Deane, Leffingwell, and Parsons not to raise our men till we came to the New Hampshire Grants, lest we should be discovered by having too long a march through the country. But when we advised with the said Easton and Brown they advised us that, as there was a great scarcity of provisions in the Grants, and as the people were generally poor, it would be difficult to get a sufficient number of men there; therefore we had better raise a number of men sooner. Said Easton and Brown concluded to go with us, and Easton said he would assist me in raising some men in his regiment. We then concluded for me to go with Col. Easton to Jericho and Williamstown to raise men, and the rest of us to go forward to Bennington and see if they could purchase provisions there.

We raised twenty-four men in Jericho and fifteen in Williamstown; got them equipped ready to march. Then Col. Easton and I set out for Bennington. That evening we met with an express for our people informing us that they had seen a man directly from Ticonderoga and he informed them that they were re-enforced at Ticonderoga, and were repairing the garrison, and were every way on their guard; therefore it was best for us to dismiss the men we had raised and proceed no further, as we should not succeed. I asked who the man was, where he belonged, and where he was going, but could get no account; on which I ordered that the men should not be dismissed, but that we should proceed. The next day I arrived at Bennington. There overtook our people, all but Mr. Noah Phelps and Mr. Heacock, who were gone forward to reconnoitre the fort: and Mr.

Halsey and Mr. Stevens had not got back from Albany.

The following account of expenses incurred on this expedition is amusing, pitiful, and interesting, as evidence of the small beginnings of the Revolution, and as compared with the machinery of transportation and the wealth of the nation in its Civil War:

Account of Captain Edward Mott for his expenses going to Ticonderoga and afterwards against the Colony of Connecticut:

	£	s.	d.
April 26th.—To expenses from Preston to Hartford......................	0	5	0
Expenses at Hartford while consulting what plan to take, or where it would be best to raise the men....	0	15	0
April 30th.—To expenses of six men at New Hartford on our way to New Hampshire Grants to raise men ($3).............................	0	18	0
May 1st.—To expenses at Norfolk ($2.50).........................	0	15	0
To expenses at Shaftsbury.....	0	7	8
To expenses in Jericho while raising men.............................	1	0	5
To expenses of marching men from Jericho to Williamstown.........	1	4	0

	£	s.	d.
May 1st.—To expenses at Allentown..	o	6	8
To expenses at Massachusetts......	2	4	6
" " " Newport............	o	16	o
" " " Pawlet.............	1	3	3
" " " Castleton..........	1	6	o
To cash to a teamster for carting provisions.....................	o	6	o
To cash to Captain Noah Phelps £1 and to Elijah Babcock £6........	7	o	o
To cash to Colonel Ethan Allen's wife...........................	3	o	o
To a horse cost me £20 in cash ($66.66), which I wore out in riding to raise the men and going to Ticonderoga, so that I was obliged to leave her and get another horse to ride back to Hartford..........................	20	o	o
To my expenses from Ticonderoga back to Hartford after we had taken the fort..................	2	o	o
To my time or wages while going on said service, and going from Hartford to Philadelphia to report to Congress by Governor Trumbull's orders, being between thirty and forty days, much of the time day and night......................	20	o	o

The 3d of May, 1775, is an eventful day. Four scenes interest us. At Albany there is hesitation. Halsey and Stevens have been there to obtain permission for the Ticonderoga expedition. The Albany committeemen are alarmed, for the proposition seems to be hazardous. What will the New York Congress think of it? Will the next Continental Congress, to meet seven days hence, approve of it? The committee write to the New York Congress for instructions, suggesting that if New York goes in for the invasion it will plunge northern New York into all the horrors of war.

A second scene is at Cambridge. The Committee of Safety, without waiting for permission from New York, decided to act. They issue a commission to Arnold without consulting the Massachusetts Congress, and authorize him to raise four hundred men in western Massachusetts and near colonies for the capture of Ticonderoga and Crown Point; they give him money and authority to seize and send military stores to Massachusetts. We can imagine Arnold quickly in the saddle, for the enterprise suits his genius.

Benedict Arnold was now thirty-five years

old; educated in the common schools, apprenticed as a druggist, fond of mischief, cruel, irritable, reckless of his reputation, ambitious and uncontrollable. As a boy he loved to maim young birds, placed broken glass where school-children would cut their feet, and enticed them with presents and then rushed out and horsewhipped them. He would cling to the arms of a large water-wheel at the grist-mill and thus pass beneath and above the water. When sixteen years of age he enlisted as a soldier, was released; enlisted again, was at Ticonderoga and other frontier forts; deserted; served out his apprenticeship, became a druggist and general merchant in New Haven; shipped horses, cattle, and provisions to the West Indies, commanded his own vessels, fought a duel with a Frenchman in the West Indies, became a bankrupt, and was suspected of dishonesty. Fertile in resource, he resumed business with energy but with the same obliquity of moral purpose.

With sixty volunteers, a few of them Yale students, marching from New Haven to Cambridge, he had an interview with Colonel Samuel H. Parsons near Hartford the 27th of April, and told him about the cannon and ammunition at Ticonderoga and the defenceless condition of that fort. Such was the man who endeavored to wrest the command of the expedition from Allen.

But the grandest scene of all on that 3d of May is the assemblage in Bennington, perhaps in the old Catamount Tavern of Stephen Fay. Allen, Warner, Robinson, Dr. Jonas Fay, Joseph Fay, Breakenridge are there with fifteen Connecticut men and thirty-nine Massachusetts men. Easton's Massachusetts men outnumber Warner's recruits, and Warner ranks third instead of second. No one dreams of any one but Allen for the leader. Easton is also complimented by being made chairman of the council. Allen with his usual energy takes the initiative and leaves the party to raise more men. He has been gone but a short time when Benedict Arnold arrives on horseback with one attendant at the hamlet and camp of Castleton. He sees Nott and other officers. They frankly communicate to him all their plans, and are in turn astounded by Arnold's claiming the right to take command of their whole force. He shows them his commission from the Committee of Safety in Cambridge, Mass. This paper gave authority to enlist men, but no more power over these men than any other American volunteers. Arnold's temper brooked no opposition. There is almost a mutiny among the men. They would go home, abandon the whole expedition which had so enkindled their enthusiasm, rather than be subject to Arnold. Whether this was owing to his domineering temper as exhibited before them, to his reputation in Connecticut as an unprincipled man, or entirely to their regard for their own officers and aversion to others, we can only conjecture. Tuesday morning this wrangling is resumed. Again the soldiers threaten to club their guns and go home. When told that they should be paid the same, although Arnold did command them, they would "damn" their pay. But Arnold suddenly started to leave this company and overtake Allen. The soldiers, knowing Allen's good-nature, as suddenly leave Castleton and follow Arnold to prevent his overpersuading Allen to yield to his arrogance.

When this stampede occurred, Nott and Phelps with Herrick were with the thirty men on the march to Skenesborough. They left the Remington camp at Castleton, and had gone nearly to Hydeville. The stampede

left all the provisions at Castleton, so that
Nott and Phelps were obliged to return to
Castleton, gather up the provisions, and follow
the main party to Ticonderoga. They arrived
in Shoreham too late to take part in the capture, but crossed the lake with Warner. This
incident deprives us of the benefit of Nott's
journal account of the capture itself, a loss to
be deplored. Some time Tuesday, somewhere
between Castleton and the lake, Allen and
Arnold met, and the scene occurred which has
been so often and so well told in romance and
history.

Within three weeks after the world-renowned
19th of April, 1775, Ethan stood in Castleton
with an old friend by his side, Gershom Beach,
of Rutland, a whig blacksmith, intelligent,
capable, and true. Besides some sixty Massachusetts and Connecticut allies, Allen is surrounded by from one to two hundred Green
Mountain Boys. More men were wanted, and
Beach was selected from the willing and eager
crowd to go, like Roderick Dhu's messenger
with the Cross of Fire, o'er hill and dale,
across brook and swamp, from Castleton to
Rutland, Pittsford, Brandon, Middlebury, and
Shoreham. The distance was sixty miles, the

time allowed twenty-four hours, the rallying-point a ravine at Hand's Point, Shoreham. Paul Revere rode on a good steed, over good roads, on a moonlight night, in a few hours. Gershom Beach went on foot, crossed Otter Creek twice, forded West Creek, East Creek, Furnace Brook, Neshobe River, Leicester River, Middlebury River, and walked through forests choked with underbrush, but at the end of the day allotted the men were warned and were hastening to the rendezvous. Then and not till then Beach threw himself on the ground and gave himself up to well-earned sleep. Let us give this hero his full meed of praise. After a few hours' rest he followed the men whom he had aroused and joined Allen.

CHAPTER VII.

CAPTURE OF TICONDEROGA.

IN the gray of the morning, Wednesday, May 10, 1775, Ethan Allen with eighty-three Green Mountain Boys crossed the lake. He frankly told his followers of the danger, but every gun was poised to dare that danger. Soon three huzzas rang out on the parade-ground of the sleeping fort. The English captain, De Laplace, not knowing that his nation had an enemy on this continent, asked innocently by what authority his surrender was demanded. Need I repeat the answer? No words in the language are more familiar than Allen's reply. The British colors were trailed before a power that had no national flag for more than two years afterward. A few hours later, that same day, the second session of the Continental Congress began at Philadelphia, the members all unaware and soon in part disapproving of this exploit of Allen's. The graphic account by

6

the hero's own pen is more life-like than that of any historian:

The first systematical and bloody attempt at Lexington to enslave America thoroughly electrified my mind, and fully determined me to take part with my country. And while I was wishing for an opportunity to signalize myself in its behalf, directions were privately sent to me from the then colony of Connecticut to raise the Green Mountain Boys, and if possible with them to surprise and take the fortress of Ticonderoga. This enterprise I cheerfully undertook; and after first guarding all the passes that led thither, to cut off all intelligence between the garrison and the country, made a forced march from Bennington and arrived at the lake opposite to Ticonderoga on the evening of the ninth day of May, 1775, with two hundred and thirty valiant Green Mountain Boys.

It was with the utmost difficulty that I procured boats to cross the lake. However, I landed eighty-three men near the garrison, and sent the boats back for the rear guard, commanded by Col. Seth Warner, but the day began to dawn and I found myself under a necessity to attack the fort before the rear could cross the lake, and, as it was viewed hazardous, I harangued the officers and soldiers in the following manner:

"Friends and fellow-soldiers, you have for a number of years past been a scourge and terror to arbitrary power. Your valor has been famed abroad and acknowledged, as appears by the advice and orders to me from the General Assembly of Connecticut to surprise and take the garrison now before us. I now propose to advance before you, and in person conduct you through the wicket-gate; for we must this morning either quit our pretensions to valor or possess ourselves of this fortress in a few minutes; and inasmuch as it is a desperate attempt which none but the bravest of men dare undertake, I do not urge it on any contrary to his will. You that will undertake voluntarily, poise your firelocks."

The men being at this time drawn up in three ranks, each poised his firelock. I ordered them to face to the right, and at the head of the centre file marched them immediately to the wicket-gate aforesaid, where I found a sentry posted who instantly snapped his fusee at me. I ran immediately toward him, and he retreated through the covered way into the parade within the garrison, gave a halloo, and ran under a bomb-proof. My party who followed me into the fort I formed on the parade in such a manner as to face the two barracks, which faced each other. The garrison being asleep, except the sentries, we gave three huzzas, which greatly surprised them. One of the sentries made a pass at one of my officers with a charge bayonet, and slightly wounded him. My first thought was to kill him with my sword, but in an instant I altered the design and fury of the blow to a slight cut on the side of the head; upon which he dropped his gun and asked quarter, which I readily granted him, and demanded of him the place where the commanding officer kept.

He showed me a pair of stairs in front of the barrack, on the west part of the garrison, which led up to a second story in said barrack, to which I immediately repaired, and ordered the commander, Captain De la Place, to come forth instantly, or I would sacrifice the whole garrison; at which the captain came immediately to the door with his breeches in his hand, when I ordered him to deliver me the fort instantly; he asked me by what authority I demanded it; I answered him, In the name of the great Jehovah and the Continental Congress. The authority of the Congress being very little known at that time, he began to speak again, but I interrupted him, and with my drawn sword over his head again demanded an immediate surrender of the garrison: with which he then complied and ordered his men to be forthwith paraded without arms, as he had given up the garrison.

In the mean time some of my officers had given orders, and in consequence thereof sundry of the barrack doors were beaten down, and about one-third of the garrison imprisoned, which consisted of the said commander, a Lieut. Feltham, a conducter of artillery, a gunner, two sergeants, and forty-four rank and file: about one hundred pieces of cannon, one thirteen-inch mortar, and a number of swords.

This surprise was carried into execution in the gray of the morning of the tenth day of May, 1775. The sun seemed to rise that morning with a superior lustre: and Ticonderoga and its dependencies smiled on its conquerors, who tossed about the flowing bowl, and wished success to Congress, and the liberty and freedom of America. Happy it was for me at that time, that the then future pages of the book of fate, which afterwards unfolded a miserable scene of two years and eight months' imprisonment, were hid from my view. But to return to my narrative. Col. Warner, with the rear guard, crossed the lake and joined me early in the morning, whom I sent off without loss of time with about one hundred men to take possession of Crown Point, which was garrisoned with a sergeant and twelve men; which he took possession of the same day, as also of upwards of one hundred pieces of cannon.

The soldierly qualities exhibited by Allen in the expedition seem to have been, first, reticence or concealment of·purpose from the enemy; second, power of commanding enthusiastic obedience from his men; third, adaptation of means to object; fourth, alacrity; and, fifth, courage. Success gave a brilliant *éclat* to this effort, which time has only served to render more brilliant.

The following letters written by Allen furnish us with additional information which makes the whole affair stand out vividly for nineteenth-century readers:

TICONDEROGA, May 11th, 1775.

To the Massachusetts Congress.

GENTLEMEN:—I have to inform you with pleasure unfelt before, that on break of day of the 10th of May, 1775, by the order of the General Assembly of the Colony of Connecticut, I took the fortress of Ticonderoga by storm. The soldiery was composed of about one hundred Green Mountain Boys and near fifty veteran soldiers from the Province of the Massachusetts Bay. The latter was under the command of Col. James Easton, who behaved with great zeal and fortitude not only in council, but in the assault. The soldiery behaved with such resistless fury, that they so terrified the King's Troops that they durst not fire on their assailants, and our soldiery was agreeably disappointed. The soldiery behaved with uncommon rancour when they leaped into the Fort: and it must be confessed that the Colonel has greatly contributed to the taking of that Fortress, as well as John Brown, Esq. Attorney at Law, who was also an able counsellor, and was personally in the attack. I expect the Colonies will maintain this Fort. As to the cannon and warlike stores, I hope they may serve the cause of liberty instead of tyranny, and I humbly implore your assistance in immediately assisting the Government of Connecticut in establishing a garrison in the reduced premises. Col. Easton will inform you at large.

From, gentlemen, your most obedient servant,

ETHAN ALLEN.

TICONDEROGA, May 12th, 1775.

To the Honorable Congress of the Province of the Massachusetts Bay or Council of War.

HONORABLE SIRS:—I make you a present of a major, a captain, and two lieutenants in the regular establishment for George the Third. I hope they may serve as ransomes for some of our friends at Boston, and particularly for Captain Brown of Rhode Island. A party of men under the command of Capt. Herrick has took possession of Skenesborough, imprisoned Major Skene, and seized a schooner of his. I expect in ten days time to have it rigged, manned, and armed with six or eight pieces of cannon, which, with the boats in our possession, I purpose to make an attack on the armed sloop of George the Third which is now cruising on Lake Champlain, and is about twice as big as the schooner. I hope in a short time to be authorized to acquaint your Honor that Lake Champlain and the fortifications thereon are subjected to the Colonies. The enterprise has been approbated by the officers and soldiery of the Green Mountain Boys, nor do I hesitate as to the success. I expect lives must be lost in the attack, as the commander of George's sloop is a man of courage, etc. I conclude Capt. Warner is by this time in possession of Crown Point, the ordnance, stores, etc. I conclude Governor Carleton will exert himself to oppose us, and command the Lake, etc. Messrs. Hickok, Halsey and Nichols have the charge of conducting the officers to Hartford. These gentlemen have been very assiduous and active in the late expedition. I depend upon your Honor's aid and assistance in a situation so contiguous to Canada. I subscribe myself your Honor's ever faithful, most obedient and humble servant,

ETHAN ALLEN,
At present Commander of Ticonderoga.

To the Honorable Jonathan Trumbull, Esq., Capt. General and Governor of the Colony of Connecticut.

CHAPTER VIII.

THE Continental Congress, affected by sinister influences, favored the removal of the stores and cannon of Ticonderoga to the south end of Lake George. Allen wrote to Congress a vigorous remonstrance. Massachusetts, New Hampshire, and Connecticut protested, and the project was abandoned. On May 29th, 1775, from Crown Point, Allen addressed the Continental Congress as follows:

An abstract of the action of Congress has just come to hand: and though it approves of the taking the fortress on Lake Champlain and the artillery, etc., I am, nevertheless, much surprised that your Honors should recommend it to us to remove the artillery to the south end of Lake George, and there to make a stand; the consequences of which must ruin the frontier settlements, which are extended at least one hundred miles to the northward from that place. Probably your Honors were not informed of those settlements, which consist of several thousand families who are seated on that tract of country called the New Hampshire Grants. Those inhabitants, by making those valuable acquisitions for the Colonies, have incensed Governor Carleton and all the ministerial party in Canada against them; and provided they should, after all their good service in behalf of their country, be neglected and left exposed, they will be of all men the most consummately miserable. . . .

If the King's troops be again in possession of Ticonderoga and Crown Point and command the Lake, the Indians and Canadians will be much more inclined to join with them and make incursions into the heart of our country. But the Colonies are now in possession and actual command of the Lake, having taken the armed sloop from George the Third, which was cruising in the Lake, also seized a schooner belonging to Major Skene at South Bay, and have armed and manned them both. . . . The Canadians (all except the noblesse) and also the Indians appear at present to be very friendly to us; and it is my humble opinion that the more vigorous the Colonies push the war against the King's troops in Canada, the more friends we shall find in that country. Provided I had but 500 men with me at St. John's (18th May) when we took the King's sloop, I would have advanced to Montreal. Nothing strengthens our friends in Canada equal to our prosperity in taking the sovereignty of Lake Champlain, and should the Colonies forthwith send an army of two or three thousand men and attack Montreal, we should have little to fear from the Canadians or Indians, and should easily make a conquest of that place, and set up the standard of liberty in the extensive province of Quebec, whose limit was enlarged purely to subvert the liberties of America. Striking such a blow would intimidate the Tory party in Canada, the same as the commencement of the war at Boston intimidated the Tories in the Colonies. They are a set of gentlemen that will not be converted by reason, but are easily wrought upon by fear.

By a council of war held on board the sloop the 27th instant, it was agreed to advance to the Point Aufere with the sloop and schooner, and a number of armed boats well manned, and there make a stand, act on the defensive, and by all means command the Lake and defend the frontiers. Point Aufere is about six miles this side of forty-five degrees north latitude, but if the wisdom of the Continental Congress should view the proposed invasion of the King's troops in Canada as premature or impolitic, nevertheless, I humbly conceive, when your Honors come to the knowledge of the before-mentioned facts, you will at least establish some advantageous situation toward the northerly part of Lake Champlain, as a frontier, instead of the south promontory of Lake George. Commanding the northerly part of the Lake, puts it in our power to work our policy with the Canadians and

Indians. We have made considerable proficiency
this way already. Sundry tribes have been to
visit us, and have returned to their tribes to use
their influence in our favor. We have just sent
Capt. Abraham Ninham, a Stockbridge Indian, as
our embassador of peace to the several tribes of
Indians in Canada. He was accompanied by Mr.
Winthrop Hoit, who has been a prisoner with the
Indians and understands their tongue. I do not
imagine, provided we command Lake Champlain,
there will be any need of a war with the Canadians
or Indians.

On June 2, 1775, Allen addressed the New
York Provincial Congress:

The pork forwarded to subsist the army, by your
Honors' direction, evinces your approbation of
the procedure; and as it was a private expedition,
and common fame reports that there are a number
of overgrown Tories in the province, your Honors
will the readier excuse me in not first taking your
advice in the matter, but the enterprises might
have been prevented by their treachery. It is
here reported that some of them have been lately
savingly converted, and that others have lost their
influence. If in those achievements there be anything honorary, the subjects of your government,
viz., the New Hampshire settlers, are justly entitled to a large share, as they had a great majority of numbers of the soldiery as well as the

command in making those acquisitions, and as your Honors justify and approve the same.

I desire and expect your Honors have, or soon will lay before the Grand Continental Congress, the great disadvantage it must inevitably be to the Colonies to evacuate Lake Champlain, and give up to the enemies of our country those invaluable acquisitions, the key of either Canada or our country, according as which party holds the same in possession and makes a proper improvement of it. The key is ours as yet, and provided the Colonies would suddenly push an army of two or three thousand men into Canada, they might make a conquest of all that would oppose them in the extensive province of Quebec, except a reinforcement from England should prevent it. Such a diversion would weaken General Gage or insure us of Canada.

I wish to God America would at this critical juncture exert herself agreeable to the indignity offered her by a tyrannical ministry. She might rise on eagle's wings, and mount up to glory, freedom, and immortal honor if she did but know and exert her strength. Fame is now hovering over her head. A vast continent must now sink to slavery, poverty, horror, and bondage, or rise to unconquerable freedom, immense wealth, inexpressible felicity, and immortal fame.

I will lay my life on it, with fifteen hundred men and a proper train of artillery I will take Montreal. Provided I could be thus furnished and if an army could command the field, it would be no insuperable difficulty to take Quebec. This object should be pursued, though it should take ten thousand men to accomplish the end proposed; for England cannot spare but a certain number of her troops, anyway, she has but a small number that are disciplined [this was months before the Hessians and other mercenaries were hired], and it is as long as it is broad the more that are sent to Quebec, the less they can send to Boston, or any other part of the continent.

Our friends in Canada can never help us until we first help them, except in a passive or inactive manner. There are now about seven hundred regular troops in Canada. I have lately had sundry conferences with the Indians; they are very friendly. Capt. Abraham Ninham, a Stockbridge Indian, and Mr. Winthrop Hoit, who has sundry years lived with the Caughnawgoes in the capacity of a prisoner and was made an adopted son to a motherly squaw of that tribe, have both been gone ten days to treat with the Indians as our embassadors of peace and friendship. I expect in a few weeks to hear from them. By them I sent a friendly letter to the Indians which Mr. Hoit can explain to them in Indian. The thing that so unites the Indians to us is our taking the sovereignty of Lake Champlain. They have wit enough to make a good bargain, and stand by the strongest side. Much the same may be said of the Canadians.

It may be thought that to push an army into Canada would be too premature and imprudent. If so, I propose to make a stand at the Isle-aux-Noix which the French fortified by intrenchment the last war, and greatly fatigued our large army to take it. It is about fifteen miles this side St. John's. Our only having it in our power thus to make incursions into Canada, might probably be the very reason why it would be unnecessary to do so, even if the Canadians should prove more refractory than I think for.

Lastly, with submission I would propose to your Honors to raise a small regiment of Rangers, which I could easily do, and that mostly in the counties of Albany and Charlotte, provided your Honors should think it expedient to grant commissions and thus regulate and put the same under pay. Probably your Honors may think this an impertinent proposal: it is truly the first favor I ever asked of the Government, and if it be granted, I shall be zealously ambitious to conduct for the best good of my country and the honor of the Government.

On June 9th Allen addressed the Massachusetts Congress:

These armed vessels are at present abundantly sufficient to command the Lake. The making these acquisitions has greatly attached the Canadians, and more especially the Indians, to our interest. They have no personal prejudice or con-

troversy with the United Colonies, but act upon
political principles, and consequently are inclined
to fall in with the strongest side. At present ours
has the appearance of it; as there are at present
but seven hundred regular troops in all the different parts of Canada. Add to this the consideration
of the imperious and haughty conduct of the troops,
which has much alienated the affections of both
the Canadians and Indians from them. Probably
there may soon be more troops from England sent
there, but at present you may rely on it that
Canada is in a weak and helpless condition. Two
or three thousand men, conducted by intrepid commanders, would at this juncture make a conquest
of the ministerial party in Canada with such additional numbers as may be supposed to vie with
the reinforcements that may be sent from England. Such a plan would make a diversion in
favor of the Massachusetts Bay, who have been too
much burdened with the calamity that should be
more general, as all partake of the salutary effects
of their valor and merit in the defence of the liberties of America. I hope, gentlemen, you will use
your influence in forwarding men, provisions, and
every article for the army that may be thought
necessary. Blankets, provisions, and powder are
scarce.

CHAPTER IX.

THE letters to the Indians and Canadians to which Allen has referred show still more clearly the vigorous policy and the adroitness which Allen displayed in the preparations for the invasion of Canada. He wrote to the Montreal merchants:

ST. JOHN's, May 18th.

To Mr. James Morrison and the Merchants that are friendly to the Cause of Liberty in Montreal.

GENTLEMEN:—I have the pleasure to acquaint you that Lakes George and Champlain, with the fortresses, artillery, etc., particularly the armed sloop of George the Third, with all water carriages of these lakes, are now in possession of the Colonies. I expect the English merchants, as well as all virtuous disposed gentlemen, will be in the interest of the Colonies. The advanced guard of the army is now at St. John's, and desire immediately to have a personal intercourse with you. Your immediate assistance as to provisions, ammunition, and spirituous liquors is wanted and forthwith expected, not as a donation, for I am empowered by the Colonies to purchase the same; and I desire you would forthwith and without further notice prepare for the use of the army those articles to the amount of five hundred pounds, and deliver the same to me at St. John's, or at least a part of it almost instantaneously, as the soldiers press on faster than provisions.

I need not inform you that my directions from the Colonies are, not to contend with or any way injure or molest the Canadians or Indians; but, on the other hand, treat them with the greatest friendship and kindness. You will be pleased to communicate the same to them, and some of you immediately visit me at this place, while others are active in delivering the provisions.

On May 24, 1775, Allen addressed a letter to the Indians of Canada:

HEADQUARTERS OF THE ARMY, CROWN POINT.

By advice of council of the officers, I recommend our trusty and well-beloved friend and brother, Capt. Abraham Ninham of Stockbridge, as our embassador of peace to our good brother Indians of the four tribes, viz., the Hocnaurigoes, the Surgaches, the Canesadaugaus and the Saint Fransawas.

Loving brothers and friends, I have to inform you that George the Third, King of England, has

made war with the English Colonies in America,
who have ever until now been his good subjects,
and sent his army and killed some of your good
friends and brothers at Boston, in the Province of
the Massachusetts Bay. Then your good brothers
in that Province, and in all the Colonies of English America, made war with King George and
have begun to kill the men of his army, and have
taken Ticonderoga and Crown Point from him, and
all the artillery, and also a great sloop which was
at St. Johns, and all the boats in the lake, and
have raised and are raising two great armies; one
is destined for Boston, and the other for the fortresses and department of Lake Champlain, to
fight the King's troops that oppose the Colonies
from Canada; and as King George's soldiers killed
our brothers and friends in a time of peace, I hope,
as Indians are good and honest men, you will not
fight for King George against your friends in
America, as they have done you no wrong, and
desire to live with you as brothers. You know it
is good for my warriors and Indians too, to kill the
Regulars, because they first began to kill our
brothers in this country without cause.

I was always a friend to Indians and have
hunted with them many times, and know how to
shoot and ambush like Indians, and am a great
hunter. I want to have your warriors come and
see me, and help me fight the King's Regular
troops. You know they stand all along close together rank and file, and my men fight so as

Indians do, and I want your warriors to join with me and my warriors like brothers and ambush the Regulars: if you will I will give you money, blankets, tomahawks, knives, paint, and anything there is in the army, just like brothers; and I will go with you into the woods to scout, and my men and your men will sleep together and eat and drink together, and fight Regulars because they first killed our brothers and will fight against us; therefore I want our brother Indians to help us fight, for I know Indians are good warriors and can fight well in the bush.

Ye know my warriors must fight, but if you, our brother Indians, do not fight on either side, we will still be friends and brothers; and you may come and hunt in our woods, and come with your canoes in the lake, and let us have venison at our forts on the lake, and have rum, bread, and what you want, and be like brothers. I have sent our friend Winthrop Hoit to treat with you on our behalf in friendship. You know him, for he has lived with you, and is your adopted son, and is a good man; Captain Ninham of Stockbridge and he will tell you about the whole matter more than I can write. I hope your warriors will come and see me. So I bid all my brother Indians farewell.

ETHAN ALLEN,
Colonel of the Green Mountain Boys.

Two days after the date of this letter Allen sent a copy of it to the Assembly of Connecticut, saying: "I thought it advisable that the Honorable Assembly should be informed of all our politicks."

Allen shows great shrewdness in adapting his letters to what he considers the aboriginal mind. Addressing the Indians constantly as brothers he appeals to their love of bush-fighting, and as regards the question of barter, to their love of rum. By his reiteration he recognizes the childish immaturity of the Indian. Far differently he addresses the Canadians, to whose reason he appeals and whose sense of justice he compliments:

TICONDEROGA, June 4.

Countrymen and Friends, the French people of Canada, greeting:

FRIENDS AND FELLOW-COUNTRYMEN: — You are undoubtedly more or less acquainted with the unnatural and unhappy controversy subsisting between Great Britain and her Colonies, the particulars of which in this letter we do not expatiate upon, but refer your considerations of the justice and equitableness thereof on the part of the Colonies, to the former knowledge that you have of this matter. We need only observe that the inhabitants of the Colonies view the controversy on their part to be justifiable in the sight of God, and all unprejudiced and honest men that

have or may have opportunity and ability to examine into the merits of it. Upon this principle
those inhabitants determine to vindicate their
cause, and maintain their natural and constitu-
tional rights and liberties at the expense of their
lives and fortunes, but have not the least disposition to injure, molest, or in any way deprive our
fellow-subjects, the Canadians, of their liberty or
property. Nor have they any design to urge war
against them; and from all intimations that the
inhabitants of the said Colonies have received
from the Canadians, it has appeared that they
were alike disposed for friendship and neutrality,
and not at all disposed to take part with the King's
troops in the present civil war against the Colonies.

We were, nevertheless, surprised to hear that a
number of about thirty Canadians attacked our
reconnoitring party consisting of four men, fired
on them, and pursued them, and obliged them to
return the fire. This is the account of the party
that has since arrived at headquarters. We
desire to know of any gentlemen Canadians the
facts of the case, as one story is good until another
is told. Our general order to the soldiery was,
that they should not, on pain of death, molest or
kill any of your people. But if it shall appear,
upon examination, that our reconnoitring party
commenced hostilities against your people, they
shall suffer agreeable to the sentence of a court-
martial; for our special orders from the Colonies
are to befriend and protect you if need be; so that

if you desire their friendship you are invited to embrace it, for nothing can be more undesirable to your friends in the Colonies, than a war with their fellow-subjects the Canadians, or with the Indians.

Hostilities have already begun; to fight with the King's troops has become a necessary and incumbent duty; the Colonies cannot avoid it. But pray, is it necessary that the Canadians and the inhabitants of the English Colonies should butcher one another? God forbid! There is no controversy subsisting between you and them. Pray let old England and the Colonies fight it out, and you, Canadians, stand by and see what an arm of flesh can do. We conclude, Saint Luke, Captain Mc-Coy, and other evil-minded persons whose interest and inclination is that the Canadians and the people of these Colonies should cut one another's throats, have inveigled some of the baser sort of your people to attack our said reconnoitring party.

Allen signed this letter as "At present the Principal Commander of the Army."

A copy of it was sent to Mr. Walker at Montreal by Mr. Jeffere. Another copy was sent to the New York Provincial Congress.

John Brown, a young lawyer of Pittsfield, Massachusetts, was the cause of Ethan Allen's long, terrible captivity. That alone justifies our curiosity to know all about him. In March, before the war, he made an eventful trip to Montreal, going along our borders, crossing the lakes, visiting Bennington, engaging two pilots, contracting with the foremost men there, spending days investigating the status of affairs in Canada as to the coming struggle. Reporting to his employers, Samuel Adams and Dr. Joseph Warren, he says that after stopping about a fortnight at Albany he was fourteen days journeying to St. John's, undergoing inconceivable hardships; the lake very high, the country for twenty miles each side under water; the ice breaking loose for miles; two days frozen in to an island; "we were glad to foot it on land;" "there is no prospect of Canada sending delegates to the Continental Congress." He speaks of his pilot, Peleg Sunderland, as "an old Indian hunter acquainted with the St. Francis Indians and their language." The other pilot was a captive many years ago among the Caughnawaga Indians. This last was Winthrop Hoit, of Bennington. These two men were famous for their familiarity with Indian ways and speech, as well as for general prowess, and their exploits in "beech-sealing" the Yorkers. Several days Sunderland and Hoit were among the

Caughnawagas, studying their manifestations of feeling toward the colonists. Brown gave letters to Thomas Walker and Blake, and pamphlets to four curés in La Prairie. He was kindly received by the local committee, who told him about Canadian politics, that Governor Carleton was no great politician, a man of sour, morose temper, and so forth. Brown wrote Adams and Warren he should not go to Quebec, "as a number of their committee are here," but "I shall tarry here some time." "I have established a channel of correspondence through the New Hampshire Grants which may be depended on." "One thing I must mention, to be kept as a profound secret. The fort at Ticonderoga must be seized as soon as possible should hostilities be committed by the King's troops. *The people on New Hampshire Grants have engaged to do this business.*" This letter was dated three weeks before the Lexington and Concord fights electrified the continent.

CHAPTER X.

ON July 27th committees of towns met at
Dorset to choose a lieutenant-colonel of the
regiment, and thus of those Green Mountain
Boys for whose organization Allen had been
so active and efficient with both the Continental and New York Congresses. Seth Warner
received forty-one of the forty-six votes cast.
Deep was Allen's chagrin and mortification,
as appears in the following letter to Governor
Trumbull:

TICONDEROGA, August 3, 1775.
HONORED SIR:—General Schuyler exerts his
utmost in building boats and making preparations
for the army to advance, as I suppose, to St.
John's, etc. We have an insufficient store of provisions for such an undertaking, though the pro-

jection is now universally approved. Provisions are hurrying forward, but not so fast as I could hope for. General Wooster's corps has not arrived. I fear there is some treachery among the New York Tory party relative to forwarding the expedition, though I am confident that the General is faithful. No troops from New York, except some officers, have arrived, though it is given out that they will soon be here. The General tells me he does not want any more troops till more provisions come to hand, which he is hurrying; and ordered the troops under General Wooster, part to be billeted in the mean while at Albany and part to mend the road from there to Lake George.

It is indeed an arduous work to furnish an army to prosecute an enterprise. In the interim, I am apprehensive, the enemy are forming one against us; witness the sailing of the transports and two men of war from Boston, as it is supposed for Quebeck. Probably, it appears that the King's Troops are discouraged of making incursions into the Province of the Massachusetts Bay. Likely they will send part of their force to overawe the Canadians, and inveigle the Indians into their interest. I fear the Colonies have been too slow in their resolutions and preparations relative to this department; but hope they may still succeed.

Notwithstanding my zeal and success in my country's cause, the old farmers on the New Hampshire Grants (who do not incline to go to war) have met in a committee meeting, and in their nomination of officers for the regiment of Green Mountain Boys (who are quickly to be raised) have wholly omitted me; but as the commissions will come from the Continental Congress, I hope they will remember me, as I desire to remain in the service, and remain your Honor's most obedient and humble servant,

ETHAN ALLEN.

To the Hon. Jona. Trumbull, Governor of the Colony of Connecticut.

N. B.—General Schuyler will transmit to your Honors a copy of the affidavits of two intelligent friends, who have just arrived from Canada. I apprehend that what they have delivered is truth. I find myself in the favor of the officers of the Army and the young Green Mountain Boys. How the old men came to reject me I cannot conceive, inasmuch as I saved them from the encroachments of New York. E. A.

This Jonathan Trumbull, be it remembered, was the original "Brother Jonathan."

Allen's first connection with the campaign in Canada is explained in his own narrative:

Early in the fall of the year, the little army under the command of the Generals Schuyler and Montgomery were ordered to advance into Canada. I was at Ticonderoga when this order arrived; and the General, with most of the field officers, requested me to attend them in the ex-

pedition; and though at that time I had no commission from Congress, yet they engaged me, that
I should be considered as an officer, the same as
though I had a commission; and should, as occasion might require, command certain detachments
of the army.   This I considered as an honorable
offer, and did not hesitate to comply with it.

September 8, 1775, from St. Therese, James
Livingston wrote to General Schuyler:

Your manifestos came to hand, and despatched
them off to the different Parishes with all possible care and expedition.   The Canadians are all
friends, and a spirit of freedom seems to reign
amongst them.   Colonel Allen, Major Brown and
myself set off this morning with a party of Canadians with intention to go to your army; but hearing of a party of Indians waiting for us the same
side of the river, we thought it most prudent to
retire in order, if possible, to raise a more considerable party of men.   We shall drop down the
River Chambly, as far as my house, where a
number of Canadians are waiting for us.

September 10, 1775, at Isle-aux-Noix, General Schuyler in his orders to Colonel Ritzemd,
who was going into Canada with five hundred
men, says:

Colonel Allen and Major Brown have orders to
request that provisions may be brought to you,

which must be punctually paid for, for which purpose I have furnished you with the sum of £318 1s. 10d. in gold.

September 15, 1775, at Isle-aux-Noix, General Schuyler received from James Livingston a report in which he says:

Yesterday morning, I sent a party each side of the river, Colonel Allen at their head, to take the vessels at Sorel, by surprise if possible. Numbers of people flock to them, and make no doubt they will carry their point. I have cut off the communication from Montreal to Chambly. We have nothing to fear here at present but a few seigneurs in the country endeavoring to raise forces. I hope Colonel Allen's presence will put a stop to it.

September 8, 1775, at Isle-aux-Noix, Schuyler writes Hancock:

I hope to hear in a day or two from Colonel Allen and Major Brown, who went to deliver my declaration.

This refers to Schuyler's address to the inhabitants of Canada, dated Isle-aux-Noix, September 5, 1775.

From Isle-aux-Noix, September 14, 1775, Ethan Allen reports to General Schuyler:

Set out from Isle-aux-Noix on the 8th instant; arrived at Chambly; found the Canadians in that vicinity friendly. They guarded me under arms night and day, escorted me through the woods as I desired, and showed me every courtesy I could wish for. The news of my being in this place excited many captains of the Militia and respectable gentlemen of the Canadians to visit and converse with me, as I gave out I was sent by General Schuyler to manifest his friendly intentions toward them, and delivered the General's written manifesto to them to the same purpose. I likewise sent a messenger to the chiefs of the Caughnawaga Indians, demanding the cause why sundry of the Indians had taken up arms against the United Colonies; they had sent two of their chiefs to me, who plead that it was contrary to the will and orders of their chiefs. The King's troops gave them rum and inveigled them to fight against General Schuyler; that they had sent their runners and ordered them to depart from St. John's, averring their friendship to the Colonies. Meanwhile the Sachems held a General Council, sent two of their Captains and some beads and a wampum belt as a lasting testimony of their friendship, and that they would not take up arms on either side. These tokens of friendship were delivered to me, agreeable to their ceremony, in a solemn manner, in the presence of a large auditory of Canadians, who approved of the league and manifested friendship to the Colonies, and testified their good-will on account of the advance of the army into Canada. Their fears (as they said) were, that our army was too weak to protect them against the severity of the English Government, as a defeat on our part would expose our friends in Canada to it. In this dilemma our friends expressed anxiety of mind. It furthermore appeared to me that many of the Canadians were watching the scale of power, whose attraction attracted them. In fine, our friends in Canada earnestly urged that General Schuyler should immediately environ St. John's, and that they would assist in cutting off the communication between St. John's and Chambly, and between these forts and Montreal. They furthermore assured me that they would help our army to provisions, etc., and that if our army did not make a conquest of the King's garrisons, they would be exposed to the resentment of the English Government, which they dreaded, and consequently the attempt of the army into Canada would be to them the greatest evil. They further told me that some of the inhabitants, that were in their hearts friendly to us, would, to extricate themselves, take up arms in favor of the Crown; and therefore, that it was of the last importance to them, as well as to us, that the army immediately attack St. John's; which would cause them to take up arms in our favor. Governor Carleton threatens the Canadians with fire and sword, except they assist him against the Colonies, and the seigneurs urge them to it.

They have withstood Carleton and them, and keep under arms throughout most of their Parishes, and are now anxiously watching the scale of power. This is the situation of affairs in Canada, according to my most painful discovery. Given under my hand, upon honor, this 14th day of September, 1775.   ETHAN ALLEN.

To his Excellency General Schuyler.

With one more letter from Allen (to General Montgomery) we will close his correspondence on the invasion of Canada, which he so strongly urged, so shrewdly planned, and yet which failed from lack of the co-operation of others:

ST. TOURS, September 20, 1775.

EXCELLENT SIR:—I am now in the Parish of St. Tours, four leagues to the south; have two hundred and fifty Canadians under arms; as I march they gather fast. These are the objects of taking the vessels in Sorel and General Carleton. These objects I pass by to assist the army besieging St. John's. If this place be taken the country is ours; if we miscarry in this, all other achievements will profit but little. I am fearful our army may be too sickly, and that the siege may be hard; therefore choose to assist in conquering St. John's, which, of consequence, conquers the whole. You may rely on it that I shall join you in about three days, with three hundred or more Canadian volunteers. I could raise one or two thousand in a

8

week's time, but will first visit the army with a less number, and if necessary will go again recruiting. Those that used to be enemies to our cause come cap in hand to me, and I swear by the Lord I can raise three times the number of our army in Canada, provided you continue the siege; all depends on that. It is the advice of the officers with me, that I speedily repair to the army. God grant you wisdom, fortitude and every accomplishment of a victorious general; the eyes of all America, nay, of Europe, are or will be on the economy of this army, and the consequences attending it. I am your most obedient humble servant,

ETHAN ALLEN.

P. S. —I have purchased six hogsheads of rum, and sent a sergeant with a small party to deliver it at headquarters. Mr. Livingston, and others under him, will provide what fresh beef you need; as to bread and flour, I am forwarding what I can. You may rely on my utmost attention to this object, as well as raising auxiliaries. I know the ground is swampy and bad for raising batteries, but pray let no object of obstructions be insurmountable. The glory of a victory, which will be attended with such important consequences, will crown all our fatigue, risks, and labors; to fail of victory will be an eternal disgrace; but to obtain it will elevate us on the wings of fame.

Yours, etc.,

ETHAN ALLEN.

On September 17th, three and a half months after Allen urged the invasion of Canada, Montgomery began the siege of St. John's. Two or three days later Warner arrived with his regiment of Green Mountain Boys. Arnold, not behind in energy and daring, captured a British sloop.

On September 24th Allen, with about eighty men, chiefly Canadians, met Major John Brown, with about two hundred Americans and Canadians, and Brown proposed to attack Montreal. It was agreed that Brown should cross the St. Lawrence that night above the city, while Allen crossed it below. Allen added about thirty English-Americans to his force and crossed. The cause of Brown's failure to meet him has never been explained. Several hundred English-Canadians and Indians with forty regular soldiers attacked Allen, and for two hours he bravely and skilfully fought a force several times larger than his own. Most of Allen's Canadian allies deserted him, and with thirty of his men he was finally captured, loaded with irons, and transported to England.

Thus, within five months, Allen, who had never before seen a battle or an army, who had never been trained as a soldier, becomes

famous by the capture of Ticonderoga; is influential in preventing the abandonment of
Ticonderoga; is foremost in the institution of
a regiment of Green Mountain Boys; is rejected by that regiment as its commanding
officer; is successful in raising the Canadians;
urges Congress to invade Canada; fails from
lack of support in his attack on Montreal; in
five short months, fame, defeat, and bitter
captivity.

Warner's announcement to Montgomery is
as follows:

LA PRAIRIE, September 27, 1775.

May it please your Honor, I have the disagreeable news to write you that Colonel Allen hath
met a defeat by a stronger force which sallied out
of the town of Montreal after he had crossed the
river about a mile below the town. I have no
certain knowledge as yet whether he is killed,
taken, or fled; but his defeat hath put the French
people into great consternation. They are much
concerned for fear of a company coming over
against us. Furthermore the Indian chiefs were
at Montreal at the time of Allen's battle, and
there were a number of Caughnawaga Indians in
the battle against Allen, and the people are very
fearful of the Indians. There were six in here
last night, I suppose sent as spies. I asked the
Indians concerning their appearing against us in

every battle; their answer to me was, that Carleton made them drunk and drove them to it; but they said they would do so no more. I should think it proper to keep a party at Longueil, and my party is not big enough to divide. If I must tarry here, I should be glad of my regiment, for my party is made up with different companies in different regiments, and my regulation is not as good as I could wish, for subordination to your orders is my pleasure. I am, sir, with submission, your humble servant, SETH WARNER.

To General Montgomery.

This moment arrived from Colonel Allen's defeat, Captain Duggan with the following intelligence: Colonel Allen is absolutely taken captive to Montreal with a few more, and about two or three killed, and about as many wounded. The living are not all come in. Something of a slaughter made among the King's troops. From yours to serve, SETH WARNER.

Schuyler, Montgomery, and Livingston, in letters written after the defeat, comment on Allen's imprudence in making the attack single-handed, but no mention is made of Brown, with whose force Allen expected to be re-enforced, and with whose help the tide of battle might have been turned and Canada's future might have been entirely changed.

CHAPTER XI.

THE story of Allen's captivity is best told in his own vivid narrative as follows:

On the morning of the 24th day of September I set out with my guard of about eighty men, from Longueuil, to go to Laprairie, from whence I determined to go to General Montgomery's camp; I had not advanced two miles before I met with Major Brown, who has since been advanced to the rank of a colonel, who desired me to halt, saying that he had something of importance to communicate to me and my confidants; upon which I halted the party and went into a house, and took a private room with him and several of my associates, where Colonel Brown proposed that, provided I would return to Longueuil and procure some canoes, so as to cross the river St. Lawrence a little north of Montreal, he would cross it a little to the south of the town, with near two hundred men, as he had boats sufficient, and that we could

make ourselves masters of Montreal. This plan
was readily approved by me and those in council,
and in consequence of which I returned to Longueuil, collected a few canoes, and added about
thirty English-Americans to my party and crossed
the river in the night of the 24th, agreeably to the
proposed plan.

My whole party at this time consisted of about
one hundred and ten men, near eighty of whom
were Canadians. We were most of the night
crossing the river, as we had so few canoes that
they had to pass and repass three times to carry
my party across. Soon after daybreak, I set a
guard between me and the town, with special orders to let no person pass or repass them, another
guard on the other end of the road with like directions; in the mean time, I reconnoitred the
best ground to make a defence, expecting Colonel
Brown's party was landed on the other side of the
town, he having the day before agreed to give
three huzzas with his men early in the morning,
which signal I was to return, that we might each
know that both parties were landed; but the sun
by this time being nearly two hours high, and the
sign failing, I began to conclude myself to be in
a præmunire, and would have crossed the river
back again, but I knew the enemy would have discovered such an attempt; and as there could not
more than one-third part of my troops cross at
a time, the other two-thirds would of course fall
into their hands. This I could not reconcile to

my own feelings as a man, much less as an officer; I therefore concluded to maintain the ground if possible and all to fare alike. In consequence of this resolution, I dispatched two messengers, one to Laprairie to Colonel Brown, and the other to L'Assomption, a French settlement, to Mr. Walker who was in our interest, requesting their speedy assistance, giving them at the same time to understand my critical situation. In the mean time, sundry persons came to my guards pretending to be friends, but were by them taken prisoners and brought to me. These I ordered to confinement until their friendship could be further confirmed; for I was jealous they were spies, as they proved to be afterward. One of the principal of them making his escape, exposed the weakness of my party, which was the final cause of my misfortune; for I have been since informed that Mr. Walker, agreeably to my desire, exerted himself, and had raised a considerable number of men for my assistance, which brought him into difficulty afterward, but upon hearing of my misfortune he disbanded them again.

The town of Montreal was in a great tumult. General Carleton and the royal party made every preparation to go on board their vessels of force, as I was afterward informed, but the spy escaped from my guard to the town occasioned an alteration in their policy and emboldened General Carleton to send the force which had there collected out against me. I had previously chosen my ground, but when I saw the number of the enemy as they sallied out of the town I perceived it would be a day of trouble, if not of rebuke; but I had no chance to flee, as Montreal was situated on an island and the St. Lawrence cut off my communication to General Montgomery's camp. I encouraged my soldiers to bravely defend themselves, that we should soon have help, and that we should be able to keep the ground if no more. This and much more I affirmed with the greatest seeming assurance, and which in reality I thought to be in some degree probable.

The enemy consisted of not more than forty regular troops, together with a mixed multitude, chiefly Canadians, with a number of English who lived in town, and some Indians; in all to the number of five hundred.

The reader will notice that most of my party were Canadians; indeed, it was a motley parcel of soldiery which composed both parties. However, the enemy began to attack from wood-piles, ditches, buildings, and such like places, at a considerable distance, and I returned the fire from a situation more than equally advantageous. The attack began between two and three o'clock in the afternoon, just before which I ordered a volunteer by the name of Richard Young, with a detachment of nine men as a flank guard, which, under the cover of the bank of the river, could not only annoy the enemy, but at the same time serve as a flank guard to the left of the main body.

The fire continued for some time on both sides; and I was confident that such a remote method of attack could not carry the ground, provided it should be continued till night; but near half the body of the enemy began to flank round to my right, upon which I ordered a volunteer by the name of John Dugan, who had lived many years in Canada and understood the French language, to detach about fifty Canadians, and post himself at an advantageous ditch which was on my right, to prevent my being surrounded. He advanced with the detachment, but instead of occupying the post made his escape, as did likewise Mr. Young upon the left, with their detachments. I soon perceived that the enemy was in possession of the ground which Dugan should have occupied. At this time I had but about forty-five men with me, some of whom were wounded; the enemy kept closing round me, nor was it in my power to prevent it; by which means my situation, which was advantageous in the first part of the attack, ceased to be so in the last; and being entirely surrounded with such vast, unequal numbers, I ordered a retreat, but found that those of the enemy who were of the country, and their Indians, could run as fast as my men, though the regulars could not. Thus I retreated near a mile, and some of the enemy with the savages kept flanking me, and others crowded hard in the rear. In fine, I expected in a very short time to try the world of spirits; for I was apprehensive that no quarter would be given to me, and therefore had determined to sell my life as dear as I could. One of the enemy's officers boldly pressing in the rear, discharged his fusee at me; the ball whistled near me, as did many others that day. I returned the salute and missed him, as running had put us both out of breath; for I concluded we were not frightened. I then saluted him with my tongue in a harsh manner, and told him that inasmuch as his numbers were so far superior to mine, I would surrender provided I could be treated with honor and be assured of a good quarter for myself and the men who were with me; and he answered I should; another officer, coming up directly after, confirmed the treaty; upon which I agreed to surrender with my party, which then consisted of thirty-one effective men and seven wounded. I ordered them to ground their arms, which they did.

The officer I capitulated with then directed me and my party to advance toward him, which was done; I handed him my sword, and in half a minute after a savage, part of whose head was shaved, being almost naked and painted, with feathers intermixed with the hair of the other side of his head, came running to me with an incredible swiftness; he seemed to advance with more than mortal speed; as he approached near me, his hellish visage was beyond all description; snakes' eyes appear innocent in comparison to his; his features distorted, malice, death, murder, and the wrath of devils and damned spirits are the emblems of his countenance, and in less than twelve feet of me, presented his firelock; at the instant of his present, I twitched the officer to whom I gave my sword between me and the savage; but he flew round with great fury, trying to single me out to shoot me without killing the officer, but by this time I was nearly as nimble as he, keeping the officer in such a position that his danger was my defence; but in less than half a minute, I was attacked by just such another imp of hell. Then I made the officer fly around with incredible velocity for a few seconds of time, when I perceived a Canadian who had lost one eye, as appeared afterward, taking my part against the savages; and in an instant an Irishman came to my assistance with a fixed bayonet, and drove away the fiends, swearing by —— he would kill them. This tragic scene composed my mind. The escaping from so awful a death made even imprisonment happy; the more so as my conquerors on the field treated me with great civility and politeness.

The regular officers said that they were very happy to see Colonel Allen. I answered them that I should rather choose to have seen them at General Montgomery's camp. The gentlemen replied that they gave full credit to what I said, and as I walked to the town, which was, as I should guess, more than two miles, a British officer walking at my right hand and one of the French noblesse at my left; the latter of which, in the action, had his eyebrow carried away by a glancing shot, but was nevertheless very merry and facetious, and no abuse was offered me till I came to the barrack yard at Montreal, where I met General Prescott, who asked me my name, which I told him; he then asked me whether I was that Colonel Allen who took Ticonderoga. I told him that I was the very man; then he shook his cane over my head, calling me many hard names, among which he frequently used the word rebel, and put himself in a great rage. I told him he would do well not to cane me, for I was not accustomed to it, and shook my fist at him, telling him that was the beetle of mortality for him if he offered to strike; upon which Captain M'Cloud of the British, pulled him by the skirt and whispered to him, as he afterward told me, to this import, that it was inconsistent with his honor to strike a prisoner. He then ordered a sergeant's command with fixed bayonets to come forward and kill thirteen Canadians who were included in the treaty aforesaid.

It cut me to the heart to see the Canadians in so hard a case, in consequence of their having been true to me; they were wringing their hands, saying their prayers, as I concluded, and expected immediate death. I therefore stepped between the executioners and the Canadians, opened my clothes, and told General Prescott to thrust his bayonet into my breast, for I was the sole cause of the Canadians taking up arms.

The guard in the mean time, rolling their eye-balls from the General to me, as though impatiently waiting his dread command to sheath their bayonets in my heart; I could however, plainly discern, that he was in a suspense and quandary about the matter; this gave me additional hopes of succeeding; for my design was not to die, but to save the Canadians by a finesse. The general stood a minute, when he made the following reply: "I will not execute you now, but you shall grace a halter at Tyburn, —— you."

I remember I disdained his mentioning such a place; I was, notwithstanding, a little pleased with the expression, as it significantly conveyed to me the idea of postponing the present appearance of death; besides, his sentence was by no means final as to "gracing a halter," although I had anxiety about it after I landed in England, as the reader will find in the course of this history. General Prescott then ordered one of his officers to take me on board the *Gaspee* schooner of war and confine me, hands and feet, in irons, which was done the same afternoon I was taken.

The action continued an hour and three-quarters by the watch, and I know not to this day how many of my men were killed, though I am certain there were but few. If I remember right, seven were wounded; one of them, Wm. Stewart by name, was wounded by a savage with a tomahawk after he was taken prisoner and disarmed, but was rescued by some of the generous enemy, and so far recovered of his wounds that he afterward went with the other prisoners to England.

Of the enemy, were killed a Major Carden, who had been wounded in eleven different battles, and an eminent merchant, Patterson, of Montreal, and some others, but I never knew their whole loss, as their accounts were different. I am apprehensive that it is rare that so much ammunition was expended and so little execution done by it; though such of my party as stood the ground, behaved with great fortitude—much exceeding that of the enemy—but were not the best of marksmen, and, I am apprehensive, were all killed or taken; the wounded were all put into the hospital at Montreal, and those that were not were put on board of different vessels in the river and shackled together by pairs, viz., two men fastened together by one handcuff being closely fixed to one wrist of each of them, and treated with the greatest severity, nay, as criminals.

I now come to the description of the irons which were put on me. The handcuff was of common size and form, but my leg irons I should imagine would weigh thirty pounds; the bar was eight feet long and very substantial; the shackles which encompassed my ankles were very tight. I was told by the officer who put them on that it was the king's plate, and I heard other of their officers say that it would weigh forty weight. The irons were so close upon my ankles, that I could not lay down in any other manner than on my back. I was put into the lowest and most wretched part of the vessel, where I got the favor of a chest to sit on; the same answered for my bed at night; and having procured some little blocks of the guard, who day and night, with fixed bayonets watched over me, to lie under each end of the large bar of my leg irons, to preserve my ankles from galling while I sat on the chest or lay back on the same, though most of the time, night and day, I sat on it; but at length having a desire to lie down on my side, which the closeness of my irons forbid, I desired the captain to loosen them for that purpose, but was denied the favor. The captain's name was Royal, who did not seem to be an ill-natured man, but oftentimes said that his express orders were to treat me with such severity, which was disagreeable to his own feelings; nor did he ever insult me, though many others who came on board did. One of the officers, by the name of Bradley, was very generous to me; he would often send me victuals from his own table; nor did a day fail, but he sent me a good drink of grog.

The reader is now invited back to the time I was put into irons. I requested the privilege to write to General Prescott, which was granted. I reminded him of the kind and generous manner of my treatment of the prisoners I took at Ticonderoga; the injustice and ungentlemanlike usage I had met with from him, and demanded better usage, but received no answer from him. I soon after wrote to General Carleton, which met the same success. In the mean while, many of those who were permitted to see me were very insulting.

I was confined in the manner I have related, on board the *Gaspee* schooner, about six weeks, during which time I was obliged to throw out plenty of extravagant language, which answered certain purposes, at that time, better than to grace a history.

To give an instance: upon being insulted, in a fit of anger, I twisted off a nail with my teeth, which I took to be a ten-penny nail; it went through the mortise of the band of my handcuff, and at the same time I swaggered over those who abused me, particularly a Doctor Dace, who told me that I was outlawed by New York, and deserved death for several years past; was at last fully ripened for the halter, and in a fair way to obtain it. When I challenged him, he excused himself, in consequence, as he said, of my being a criminal; but I flung such a flood of language at him that it shocked him and the spectators, for my anger was very great. I heard one say, " Him! he can eat iron! " After that, a small padlock was fixed to the handcuff instead of the nail, and as they were mean-spirited in their treatment to me, so it appeared to me that they were equally timorous and cowardly.

I was after sent with the prisoners taken with me to an armed vessel in the river, which lay off

9

against Quebec under the command of Captain
M'Cloud of the British, who treated me in a very
generous and obliging manner, and according to
my rank; in about twenty-four hours I bid him
farewell with regret, but my good fortune still
continued.   The name of the captain of the vessel I was put on board was Littlejohn, who with
his officers behaved in a polite, generous, and
friendly manner.   I lived with them in the cabin
and fared on the best, my irons being taken off,
contrary to the order he had received from the
commanding officer, but Captain Littlejohn swore
that a brave man should not be used as a rascal
on board his ship.

That I found myself in possession of happiness
once more, and the evils I had lately suffered
gave me an uncommon relish for it.

Captain Littlejohn used to go to Quebec almost
every day in order to pay his respects to certain
gentlemen and ladies; being there on a certain
day, he happened to meet with some disagreeable
treatment as he imagined, from a Lieutenant of a
man-of-war and one word brought on another, until the Lieutenant challenged him to a duel on the
plains of Abraham.   Captain Littlejohn was a
gentleman, who entertained a high sense of honor,
and could do no less than accept the challenge.

At nine o'clock the next morning they were to
fight.   The captain returned in the evening, and
acquainted his lieutenant and me with the affair.
His lieutenant was a high-blooded Scotchman, as

well as himself, who replied to his captain that
he should not want for a second. With this I interrupted him and gave the captain to understand
that since an opportunity had presented, I would
be glad to testify my gratitude to him by acting
the part of a faithful second; on which he gave
me his hand, and said that he wanted no better
man. Says he, I am a king's officer, and you a
prisoner under my care; you must therefore go
with me to the place appointed in disguise, and
added further: "You must engage me, upon the
honor of a gentleman, that whether I die or live,
or whatever happens, provided you live, that you
will return to my lieutenant on board this ship."
All this I solemnly engaged him. The comba-
tants were to discharge each a pocket pistol, and
then to fall on with their iron-hilted muckle
whangers, and one of that sort was allotted for
me; but some British officers, who interposed
early in the morning, settled the controversy without fighting.

Now having enjoyed eight or nine days' happiness from the polite and generous treatment of
Captain Littlejohn and his officers, I was obliged
to bid them farewell, parting with them in as
friendly a manner as we had lived together, which,
to the best of my memory, was the eleventh of
November; when a detachment of General Arnold's little army appeared on Point Levi, opposite Quebec, who had performed an extraordinary
march through a wilderness country with design

to have surprised the capital of Canada; I was then taken on board a vessel called the *Adamant*, together with the prisoners taken with me, and put under the power of an English merchant from London, whose name was Brook Watson; a man of malicious and cruel disposition, and who was probably excited, in the exercise of his malevolence, by a junto of tories who sailed with him to England; among whom were Colonel Guy Johnson, Colonel Closs, and their attendants and associates, to the number of about thirty.

All the ship's crew, Colonel Closs in his personal behavior excepted, behaved toward the prisoners with that spirit of bitterness which is the peculiar characteristic of tories when they have the friends of America in their power, measuring their loyalty to the English king by the barbarity, fraud and deceit which they exercised toward the whigs.

A small place in the vessel, inclosed with white-oak plank, was assigned for the prisoners, and for me among the rest. I should imagine that it was not more than twenty feet one way, and twenty-two the other. Into this place we were all, to the number of thirty-four, thrust and handcuffed, two prisoners more being added to our number, and were provided with two excrement tubs; in this circumference we were obliged to eat and perform the offices of evacuation during the voyage to England, and were insulted by every blackguard sailor and tory on board, in the cruellest manner;

but what is the most surprising thing is, that not one, of us died in the passage. When I was first ordered to go into the filthy inclosure, through a small sort of door, I positively refused, and endeavored to reason the before-named Brook Watson out of a conduct so derogatory to every sentiment of honor and humanity, but all to no purpose, my men being forced in the den already; and the rascal who had the charge of the prisoners commanded me to go immediately in among the rest. He further added, that the place was good enough for a rebel; that it was impertinent for a capital offender to talk of honor or humanity; that anything short of a halter was too good for me, and that would be my portion soon after I landed in England, for which purpose only I was sent thither. About the same time a lieutenant among the tories insulted me in a grievous manner, saying I ought to have been executed for my rebellion against New York, and spit in my face, upon which, though I was in handcuffs, I sprang at him with both hands and knocked him partly down, but he scrambled along into the cabin, and I after him; there he got under the protection of some men with fixed bayonets, who were ordered to make ready to drive me into the place aforementioned. I challenged him to fight, notwithstanding the impediments that were on my hands, and had the exalted pleasure to see the rascal tremble for fear; his name I have forgot, but Watson ordered his guard to get me into the place with the other prisoners, dead or alive; and I had almost as lieve died as do it, standing it out till they environed me round with bayonets, and brutish, prejudiced, abandoned wretches they were, from whom I could expect nothing but wounds or death; however, I told them that they were good honest fellows, that I could not blame them; that I was only in dispute with a calico merchant, who knew not how to behave toward a gentleman of the military establishment. This was spoken rather to appease them for my own preservation, as well as to treat Watson with contempt; but still I found they were determined to force me into the wretched circumstances, which their prejudiced and depraved minds had prepared for me; therefore, rather than die I submitted to their indignities, being drove with bayonets into the filthy dungeon with the other prisoners, where we were denied fresh water, except a small allowance, which was very inadequate to our wants; and in consequence of the stench of the place, each of us was soon followed with a diarrhœa and fever, which occasioned intolerable thirst. When we asked for water, we were, most commonly, instead of obtaining it, insulted and derided; and to add to all the horrors of the place, it was so dark that we could not see each other, and were overspread with body-lice. We had, notwithstanding these severities, full allowance of salt provisions, and a gill of rum per day; the latter of which was of the utmost service to us, and, probably, was the means of saving several of our lives. About forty days we existed in this manner, when the land's end of England was discovered from the mast head; soon after which, the prisoners were taken from their gloomy abode, being permitted to see the light of the sun, and breathe fresh air, which to us was very refreshing. The day following we landed at Falmouth.

A few days before I was taken prisoner I shifted my clothes, by which I happened to be taken in a Canadian dress, viz., a short fawn-skin jacket, double breasted, an undervest and breeches of sagathy, worsted stockings, a decent pair of shoes, two plain shirts, and a red worsted cap; this was all the clothing I had, in which I made my appearance in England.

When the prisoners were landed, multitudes of the citizens of Falmouth, excited by curiosity, crowded to see us, which was equally gratifying to us. I saw numbers on the house tops and the rising adjacent grounds were covered with them, of both sexes. The throng was so great, that the king's officers were obliged to draw their swords, and force a passage to Pendennis castle, which was near a mile from the town, where we were closely confined, in consequence of orders from General Carleton, who then commanded in Canada.

CHAPTER XII.

THE rascally Brook Watson then set out for London in great haste, expecting the reward of his zeal; but the ministry received him, as I have been since informed, rather coolly; but the minority in parliament took advantage, arguing that the opposition of America to Great Britain was not a rebellion. If it is, say they, why do you not execute Colonel Allen according to law? but the majority argued that I ought to be executed, and that the opposition was really a rebellion, but that policy obliged them not to do it, inasmuch as the congress had then most prisoners in their power; so that my being sent to England, for the purpose of being executed, and necessity restraining them, was rather a foil on their laws and authority, and they consequently disapproved of my being sent thither. But I had never heard the least hint of those debates in parliament, or of the working of their policy, until some time after I left England.

Consequently the reader will readily conceive I was anxious about my preservation, knowing that

I was in the power of a haughty and cruel nation considered as such. Therefore, the first proposition which I determined in my own mind was, that humanity and moral suasion would not be consulted in the determining of my fate; and those that daily came in great numbers out of curiosity to see me, both gentle and simple, united in this, that I would be hanged. A gentleman from America, by the name of Temple, and who was friendly to me, just whispered to me in the ear, and told me that bets were laid in London, that I would be executed; he likewise privately gave me a guinea, but durst say but little to me.

However, agreeably to my first negative proposition, that moral virtue would not influence my destiny, I had recourse to stratagem, which I was in hopes would move in the circle of their policy. I requested of the commander of the castle, the privilege of writing to congress, who, after consulting with an officer that lived in town, of a superior rank, permitted me to write. I wrote in the fore part of the letter, a short narrative of my ill-treatment; but withal let them know that, though I was treated as a criminal in England, and continued in irons, together with those taken with me, yet it was, in consequence of the orders which the commander of the castle received from General Carleton, and therefore desired congress to desist from matters of retaliation, until they should know the result of the government in England respecting their treatment toward me, and the prisoners with me, and govern themselves accordingly, with a particular request that, if retaliation should be found necessary, it might be exercised not according to the smallness of my character in America, but in proportion to the importance of the cause for which I suffered. This is, according to my present recollection, the substance of the letter inscribed: "To the illustrious Continental Congress." This letter was written with the view that it should be sent to the ministry at London, rather than to congress, with a design to intimidate the haughty English government, and screen my neck from the halter.

The next day the officer, from whom I obtained license to write, came to see me and frowned on me on account of the impudence of the letter, as he phrased it, and further added, "Do you think that we are fools in England, and would send your letter to congress, with instructions to retaliate on our own people? I have sent your letter to Lord North." This gave me inward satisfaction, though I carefully concealed it with a pretended resentment, for I found that I had come Yankee over him, and that the letter had gone to the identical person I designed it for. Nor do I know to this day, but that it had the desired effect, though I have not heard anything of the letter since.

My personal treatment by Lieutenant Hamilton, who commanded the castle, was very generous. He sent me every day a fine breakfast and dinner from his own table, and a bottle of good wine.

Another aged gentleman, whose name I cannot recollect, sent me a good supper. . But there was no
distinction between me and the privates; we all
lodged in a sort of Dutch bunks, in one common
apartment, and were allowed straw. The privates
were well supplied with provisions, and with me,
took effectual measures to rid themselves of lice.

I could not but feel, inwardly, extremely anxious
for my fate. This I, however, concealed from the
prisoners, as well as from the enemy, who were
perpetually shaking the halter at me. I nevertheless treated them with scorn and contempt; and
having sent my letter to the ministry, could conceive of nothing more in my power but to keep up
my spirits, behave in a daring, soldier-like manner, that I might exhibit a good sample of American fortitude. Such a conduct, I judged, would
have a more probable tendency to my preservation
than concession and timidity. This, therefore,
was my deportment: and I had lastly determined
in my mind, that if a cruel death must inevitably
be my portion, I would face it undaunted; and
though I greatly rejoice that I returned to my
country and friends, and to see the power and
pride of Great Britain humbled, yet I am confident I could then have died without the least appearance of dismay.

I now clearly recollect that my mind was so resolved that I would not have trembled or shown
the least fear, as I was sensible that it could not
alter my fate, nor do more than reproach my

memory, make my last act despicable to my
enemies, and eclipse the other actions of my life.
For I reasoned thus, that nothing was more common than for men to die with their friends around
them, weeping and lamenting over them, but not
able to help them, which was in reality not different in the consequence of it from such a death as
I was apprehensive of; and as death was the natural consequence of animal life to which the laws
of nature subject mankind, to be timorous and un-
easy as to the event and manner of it was inconsistent with the character of a philosopher and
soldier. The cause I was engaged in I ever viewed
worthy hazarding my life for, nor was I, in the
most critical moments of trouble, sorry that I engaged in it; and as to the world of spirits, though
I knew nothing of the mode or manner of it, I expected nevertheless, when I should arrive at such
a world, that I should be as well treated as other
gentlemen of my merit.

Among the great numbers of people who came
to the castle to see the prisoners, some gentlemen
told me that they had come fifty miles on purpose
to see me, and desired to ask me a number of
questions, and to make free with me in conversation. I gave for answer that I chose freedom in
every sense of the word. Then one of them asked
me what my occupation in life had been. I answered him, that in my younger days I had studied
divinity but was a conjuror by profession. He
replied that I conjured wrong at the time I was

taken; and I was obliged to own that I mistook a figure at that time, but that I had conjured them out of Ticonderoga. This was a place of great notoriety in England, so that the joke seemed to go in my favor.

It was a common thing for me to be taken out of close confinement, into a spacious green in the castle, or rather parade, where numbers of gentlemen and ladies were ready to see and hear me. I often entertained such audiences with harangues on the impracticability of Great Britain's conquering the colonies of America. At one of these times I asked a gentleman for a bowl of punch, and he ordered his servant to bring it, which he did, and offered it to me, but I refused to take it from the hand of his servant; he then gave it to me with his own hand, refusing to drink with me in consequence of my being a state criminal. However, I took the punch and drank it all down at one draught, and handed the gentleman the bowl; this made the spectators as well as myself merry.

I expatiated on American freedom. This gained the resentment of a young beardless gentleman of the company, who gave himself very great airs, and replied that he knew the Americans very well, and was certain thy could not bear the smell of powder. I replied that I accepted it as a challenge, and was ready to convince him on the spot that an American could bear the smell of powder; at which he answered that he should not put himself on a par with me. I then demanded him to treat the character of the Americans with due respect. He answered that I was an Irishman; but I assured him that I was a full-blooded Yankee, and in fine bantered him so much, that he left me in possession of the ground, and the laugh went against him. Two clergymen came to see me, and inasmuch as they behaved with civility, I returned them the same. We discoursed on several parts of moral philosophy and Christianity; and they seemed to be surprised that I should be acquainted with such topics, or that I should understand a syllogism or regular mode of argumentation. I am apprehensive my Canadian dress contributed not a little to the surprise and excitement of curiosity: to see a gentleman in England regularly dressed and well behaved would be no sight at all; but such a rebel as they were pleased to call me, it is probable, was never before seen in England.

The prisoners were landed at Falmouth a few days before Christmas, and ordered on board of the *Solebay* frigate, Captain Symonds, on the eighth day of January, 1776, when our hand irons were taken off. This remove was in consequence, as I have been since informed, of a writ of habeas corpus, which had been procured by some gentlemen in England, in order to obtain me my liberty.

The *Solebay*, with sundry other men-of-war and about forty transports, rendezvoused at the cove of Cork, in Ireland, to take in provisions and water.

When we were first brought on board, Captain Symonds ordered all the prisoners and most of the hands on board to go on the deck, and caused to be read in their hearing a certain code of laws or rules for the regulation and ordering of their behavior; and then in a sovereign manner, ordered the prisoners, me in particular, off the deck and never to come on it again: for, said he, this is a place for gentlemen to walk. So I went off, an officer following me, who told me he would show me the place allotted to me, and took me down to the cabin tier, saying to me this is your place.

Prior to this I had taken cold, by which I was in an ill state of health, and did not say much to the officer; but stayed there that night, consulted my policy, and I found I was in an evil case: that a captain of a man-of-war was more arbitrary than a king, as he could view his territory with a look of his eye, and a movement of his finger commanded obedience. I felt myself more desponding than I had done at any time before; for I concluded it to be a government scheme, to do that clandestinely which policy forbid to be done under sanction of any public justice and law.

However, two days after, I shaved and cleansed myself as well as I could, and went on deck. The captain spoke to me in a great rage, and said: "Did I not order you not to come on deck?" I answered him, that at the same time he said, "that it was the place for gentlemen to walk; that I was Colonel Allen, but had not been properly introduced to him." He replied, "—— —— you, sir, be careful not to walk the same side of the deck that I do." This gave me encouragement, and ever after that I walked in the manner he had directed, except when he, at certain times afterward, had ordered me off in a passion, and I then would directly afterward go on again, telling him to command his slaves; that I was a gentleman and had a right to walk the deck; yet when he expressly ordered me off I obeyed, not out of obedience to him, but to set an example to the ship's crew, who ought to obey him.

To walk to the windward side of the deck is, according to custom, the prerogative of the captain of the man-of-war, though he, sometimes, nay commonly, walks with his lieutenants, when no . strangers are by. When a captain from some other man-of-war comes on board, the captains walk to the windward side, and the other gentlemen to the leeward.

It was but a few nights I lodged in the cabin tier before I gained an acquaintance with the master of arms; his name was Gillegan, an Irishman, who was a generous and well-disposed man, and in a friendly manner made me an offer of living with him in a little berth, which was allotted him between decks, and inclosed in canvas; his preferment on board was about equal to that of a sergeant in a regiment. I was comparatively happy in the acceptance of his clemency, and lived with him in friendship till the frigate anchored in the harbor of Cape Fear, North Carolina, in America.

Nothing of material consequence happened till the fleet rendezvoused at the cove of Cork, except a violent storm which brought old hardy sailors to their prayers. It was soon rumored in Cork that I was on board the *Solebay*, with a number of prisoners from America, upon which Messrs. Clark & Hays, merchants in company, and a number of other benevolently disposed gentlemen, contributed largely to the relief and support of the prisoners, who were thirty-four in number, and in very needy circumstances. A suit of clothes from head to foot, including an overcoat or surtout, and two shirts were bestowed upon each of them. My suit I received in superfine broadcloth, sufficient for two jackets and two pairs of breeches, overplus of a suit throughout, eight fine Holland shirts and socks ready made, with a number of pairs of silk and worsted hose, two pairs of shoes, two beaver hats, one of which was sent me, richly laced with gold, by James Bonwell. The Irish gentlemen furthermore made a large gratuity of wines of the best sort, spirits, gin, loaf and brown sugar, tea and chocolate, with a large round of pickled beef, and a number of fat turkies, with many other articles, for my sea stores, too tedious to mention here. To the privates they bestowed on each man two pounds of tea and six pounds of brown sugar. These articles were received on board at a time when the captain and first lieuten-

10

ant were gone on shore, by the permission of the second lieutenant, a handsome young gentleman, who was then under twenty-one years of age; his name was Douglass, son of Admiral Douglass, as I was informed.

As this munificence was so unexpected and plentiful, I may add needful, it impressed on my mind the highest sense of gratitude toward my benefactors; for I was not only supplied with the necessaries and conveniences of life, but with the grandeurs and superfluities of it. Mr. Hays, one of the donators before-mentioned, came on board and behaved in the most obliging manner, telling me that he hoped my troubles were past, for that the gentlemen of Cork determined to make my sea stores equal to that of the captain of the *Solebay ;* he made an offer of live-stock and wherewith to support them; but I knew this would be denied. And to crown all, did send me by another person fifty guineas, but I could not reconcile receiving the whole to my own feelings, as it might have the appearance of avarice, and therefore received but seven guineas only, and am confident, not only from the exercises of the present well-timed generosity, but from a large acquaintance with gentlemen of this nation, that as a people they excel in liberality and bravery.

Two days after the receipt of the aforesaid donations, Captain Symonds came on board full of envy toward the prisoners, and swore by all that is good that the damned American rebels should not be feasted at this rate by the damned rebels of Ireland; he therefore took away all my liquors before-mentioned, except some of the wine which was secreted, and a two-gallon jug of old spirits which was reserved for me per favor of Lieutenant Douglass. The taking of my liquors was abominable in his sight. He therefore spoke in my behalf, till the captain was angry with him, and in consequence proceeded and took away all the tea and sugar which had been given to the prisoners, and confiscated it to the use of the ship's crew. Our clothing was not taken away, but the privates were forced to do duty on board. Soon after this there came a boat to the side of the ship and Captain Symonds asked a gentleman in it, in my hearing, what his business was, who answered that he was sent to deliver some sea stores to Colonel Allen, which, if I remember right, he said were sent from Dublin; but the captain damned him heartily, ordering him away from the ship, and would not suffer him to deliver the stores. I was furthermore informed that the gentlemen in Cork requested of Captain Symonds that I might be allowed to come into the city, and that they would be responsible I should return to the frigate at a given time, which was denied them.

We sailed from England on the 8th day of January, and from the cove of Cork on the 12th day of February. Just before we sailed, the prisoners with me were divided and put on board three different ships of war. This gave me some uneasiness, for they were to a man zealous in the cause of liberty, and behaved with a becoming fortitude in the various scenes of their captivity; but those who were distributed on board other ships of war were much better used than those who tarried with me, as appeared afterward. When the fleet, consisting of about forty-five sail, including five men-of-war, sailed from the cove with a fresh breeze, the appearance was beautiful, abstracted from the unjust and bloody designs they had in view. We had not sailed many days before a mighty storm arose, which lasted near twenty-four hours without intermission. The wind blew with relentless fury, and no man could remain on deck, except he was lashed fast, for the waves rolled over the deck by turns, with a forcible rapidity, and every soul on board was anxious for the preservation of the ship, alias their lives. In this storm the *Thunder-bomb* man-of-war sprang aleak, and was afterward floated to some part of the coast of England, and the crew saved. We were then said to be in the Bay of Biscay. After the storm abated, I could plainly discern the prisoners were better used for some considerable time.

Nothing of consequence happened after this, till we sailed to the island of Madeira, except a certain favor I had received of Captain Symonds, in consequence of an application I made to him for the privilege of his tailor to make me a suit of clothes of the cloth bestowed on me in Ireland,

which he generously granted. I could then walk
the deck with a seeming better grace. When we
had reached Madeira and anchored, sundry gentlemen with the captain went on shore, who, I
conclude, gave the rumor that I was in the frigate,
upon which I soon found that Irish generosity was
again excited; for a gentleman of that nation sent
his clerk on board to know of me if I could accept a sea store from him, particularly wine. This
matter I made known to the generous Lieutenant
Douglass, who readily granted me the favor, provided the articles could be brought on board during the time of his command; adding that it would
be a pleasure to him to serve me, notwithstanding
the opposition he met with before. So I directed
the gentleman's clerk to inform him that I was
greatly in need of so signal a charity, and desired
the young gentleman to make the utmost dispatch,
which he did; but in the mean time Captain Symonds and his officers came on board, and immediately made ready for sailing; the wind at the
same time being fair, set sail when the young
gentleman was in fair sight with the aforesaid
store.

The reader will doubtless recollect the seven
guineas I received at the cove of Cork. These
enabled me to purchase of the purser what I
wanted, had not the captain strictly forbidden it,
though I made sundry applications to him for that
purpose; but his answer to me, when I was sick,
was, that it was no matter how soon I was dead,

and that he was no ways anxious to preserve the lives of rebels, but wished them all dead; and indeed that was the language of most of the ship's crew. I expostulated not only with the captain, but with other gentlemen on board, on the unreasonableness of such usage; inferring that inasmuch as the government in England did not proceed against me as a capital offender, they should not; for that they were by no means empowered by any authority, either civil or military, to do so; for the English government had acquitted me by sending me back a prisoner of war to America, and that they should treat me as such. I further drew an inference of impolicy on them, provided they should by hard usage destroy my life; inasmuch as I might, if living, redeem one of their officers; but the captain replied that he needed no directions of mine how to treat a rebel; that the British would conquer the American rebels, hang the Congress and such as promoted the rebellion, me in particular, and retake their own prisoners; so that my life was of no consequence in the scale of their policy. I gave him for answer that if they stayed till they conquered America before they hanged me, I should die of old age, and desired that till such an event took place, he would at least allow me to purchase of the purser, for my own money, such articles as I greatly needed; but he would not permit it, and when I reminded him of the generous and civil usage that their prisoners in captivity in America met with, he said that it was not owing to their goodness, but to their timidity; for, said he, they expect to be conquered, and therefore dare not misuse our prisoners; and in fact this was the language of the British officers till Burgoyne was taken; happy event! and not only of the officers but the whole British army. I appeal to all my brother prisoners who have been with the British in the southern department for a confirmation of what I have advanced on this subject. The surgeon of the *Solebay*, whose name was North, was a very humane, obliging man, and took the best care of the prisoners who were sick.

CHAPTER XIII.

THE third day of May we cast anchor in the harbor of Cape Fear, in North Carolina, as did Sir Peter Parker's ship, of fifty guns, a little back of the bar; for there was not depth of water for him to come into the harbor. These two men-of-war, and fourteen sail of transports and others, came after, so that most of the fleet rendezvoused at Cape Fear for three weeks. The soldiers on board the transports were sickly, in consequence of so long a passage; add to this the small-pox carried off many of them. They landed on the main, and formed a camp; but the riflemen annoyed them, and caused them to move to an island in the harbor; but such cursing of riflemen I never heard.

A detachment of regulars was sent up Brunswick River; as they landed they were fired on by those marksmen, and they came back next day damning the rebels for their unmanly way of fighting, and swearing they would give no quarter, for they took sight at them, and were behind tim-

ber, skulking about. One of the detachments said
they lost one man; but a negro man who was with
them, and heard what was said, soon after told me
that he helped to bury thirty-one of them; this
did me some good to find my countrymen giving
them battle; for I never heard such swaggering
as among General Clinton's little army, who commanded at that time; and I am apt to think there
were four thousand men, though not two-thirds of
them fit for duty. I heard numbers of them say
that the trees in America should hang well with
fruit that campaign, for they would give no quarter. This was in the mouths of most who I heard
speak on the subject, officer as well as soldier. I
wished at that time my countrymen knew, as
well as I did, what a murdering and cruel enemy
they had to deal with; but experience has since
taught this country what they are to expect at the
hands of Britons when in their power.

The prisoners who had been sent on board different men-of-war at the cove of Cork were collected together, and the whole of them put on
board the *Mercury* frigate, Captain James Montague, except one of the Canadians, who died on the
passage from Ireland, and Peter Noble, who made
his escape from the *Sphynx* man-of-war in this
harbor, and, by extraordinary swimming, got safe
home to New England and gave intelligence of
the usage of his brother prisoners. The *Mercury*
set sail from this port for Halifax about the 20th
of May, and Sir Peter Parker was about to sail

with the land forces, under the command of General Clinton, for the reduction of Charleston, the capital of South Carolina, and when I heard of his defeat in Halifax, it gave me inexpressible satisfaction.

I now found myself under a worse captain than Symonds; for Montague was loaded with prejudices against everybody and everything that was not stamped with royalty; and being by nature underwitted, his wrath was heavier than the others, or at least his mind was in no instance liable to be diverted by good sense, humor or bravery, of which Symonds was by turns susceptible. A Captain Francis Proctor was added to our number of prisoners when we were first put on board this ship. This gentleman had formerly belonged to the English service. The captain, and in fine, all the gentlemen of the ship were very much incensed against him, and put him in irons without the least provocation, and he was continued in this miserable situation about three months. In this passage the prisoners were infected with the scurvy, some more and some less, but most of them severely. The ship's crew was to a great degree troubled with it, and I concluded it was catching. Several of the crew died with it on their passage. I was weak and feeble in consequence of so long and cruel a captivity, yet had but little of the scurvy.

The purser was again expressly forbid by the captain to let me have anything out of his store;

upon which I went upon deck, and in the handsomest manner requested the favor of purchasing a few necessaries of the purser, which was denied me; he further told me, that I should be hanged as soon as I arrived at Halifax. I tried to reason the matter with him, but found him proof against reason; I also held up his honor to view, and his behavior to me and the prisoners in general, as being derogatory to it, but found his honor impenetrable. I then endeavored to touch his humanity, but found he had none; for his prepossession of bigotry to his own party had confirmed him in an opinion that no humanity was due to unroyalists, but seemed to think that heaven and earth were made merely to gratify the king and his creatures; he uttered considerable unintelligible and grovelling ideas, a little tinctured with monarchy but stood well to his text of hanging me. He afterward forbade his surgeon to administer any help to the sick prisoners. I was every night shut down in the cable tier with the rest of the prisoners, and we all lived miserably while under his power. But I received some generosity from several of the midshipmen who in degree alleviated my misery; one of their names was Putrass; the names of the others I do not recollect; but they were obliged to be private in the bestowment of their favor, which was sometimes good wine bitters and at others a generous drink of grog.

Some time in the first week of June, we came to

anchor at the Hook of New York, where we remained but three days; in which time Governor Tryon, Mr. Kemp, the old attorney-general of New York, and several other perfidious and overgrown tories and land-jobbers, came on board. Tryon viewed me with a stern countenance, as I was walking on the leeward side of the deck with the midshipmen; and he and his companions were walking with the captain and lieutenant on the windward side of the same, but never spoke to me, though it is altogether probable that he thought of the old quarrel between him, the old government of New York, and the Green Mountain Boys. Then they went with the captain into the cabin, and the same afternoon returned on board a vessel, where at that time they took sanctuary from the resentment of their injured country. What passed between the officers of the ship and these visitors I know not; but this I know, that my treatment from the officers was more severe afterward.

We arrived at Halifax not far from the middle of June, where the ship's crew, which was infested with the scurvy, were taken on shore and shallow trenches dug, into which they were put, and partly covered with earth. Indeed, every proper measure was taken for their relief. The prisoners were not permitted any sort of medicine, but were put on board a sloop which lay in the harbor, near the town of Halifax, surrounded by several men-of-war and their tenders, and a guard constantly set over them, night and day. The sloop we had wholly to ourselves, except the guard who occupied the forecastle; here we were cruelly pinched with hunger; it seemed to me that we had not more than one-third of the common allowance. We were all seized with violent hunger and faintness; we divided our scanty allowance as exact as possible. I shared the same fate with the rest, and though they offered me more than an even share, I refused to accept it, as it was a time of substantial distress, which in my opinion I ought to partake equally with the rest, and set an example of virtue and fortitude to our little commonwealth.

I sent letter after letter to Captain Montague, who still had the care of us, and also to his lieutenant, whose name I cannot call to mind, but could obtain no answer, much less a redress of grievances; and to add to the calamity, nearly a dozen of the prisoners were dangerously ill of the scurvy. I wrote private letters to the doctors, to procure, if possible, some remedy for the sick, but in vain. The chief physician came by in a boat, so close that the oars touched the sloop that we were in, and I uttered my complaint in the genteelest manner to him, but he never so much as turned his head, or made me any answer, though I continued speaking till he got out of hearing. Our cause then became deplorable. Still I kept writing to the captain, till he ordered the guards, as they told me, not to bring any more letters from me to him. In the mean time an event happened worth relating. One of the men, almost dead with the scurvy, lay by the side of the sloop, and a canoe of Indians coming by, he purchased two quarts of strawberries, and ate them at once, and it almost cured him. The money he gave for them was all the money he had in the world. After that we tried every way to procure more of that fruit, reasoning from analogy that they might have the same effect on others infested with the same disease, but could obtain none.

Meanwhile the doctor's mate of the *Mercury* came privately on board the prison sloop and presented me with a large vial of smart drops, which proved to be good for the scurvy, though vegetables and some other ingredients were requisite for a cure: but the drops gave at least a check to the disease. This was a well-timed exertion of humanity, but the doctor's name has slipped my mind, and in my opinion, it was the means of saving the lives of several men.

The guard which was set over us was by this time touched with feelings of compassion; and I finally trusted one of them with a letter of complaint to Governor Arbuthnot, of Halifax, which he found means to communicate, and which had the desired effect; for the governor sent an officer and surgeon on board the prison sloop to know the truth of the complaint. The officer's name was Russell; he held the rank of lieutenant, and treated me in a friendly and polite manner, and was really angry at the cruel and unmanly usage the prisoners met with; and with the surgeon

made a true report of matters to Governor Arbuthnot, who, either by his order or influence, took us
next day from the prison sloop to Halifax jail,
where I first became acquainted with the now
Hon. James Lovel, one of the members of Congress for the State of Massachusetts. The sick
were taken to the hospital, and the Canadians,
who were effective, were employed in the king's
works; and when their countrymen were recovered
from the scurvy and joined them, they all deserted
the king's employ, and were not heard of at Halifax as long as the remainder of the prisoners continued there, which was till near the middle of
October. We were on board the prison sloop
about six weeks, and were landed at Halifax near
the middle of August. Several of our English-
American prisoners, who were cured of the scurvy
at the hospital, made their escape from thence,
and after a long time reached their old habitations.

I had now but thirteen with me of those who
were taken in Canada, and remained in jail with
me at Halifax, who, in addition to those that were
imprisoned before, made our number about thirty-
four, who were all locked up in one common large
room, without regard to rank, education, or any
other accomplishment, where we continued from
the setting to the rising sun; and as sundry of
them were infected with the jail and other dis-
tempers, the furniture of this spacious room consisted principally of excrement tubs. We petitioned for a removal of the sick into the hospitals,

but were denied. We remonstrated against the ungenerous usage of being confined with the privates, as being contrary to the laws and customs of nations, and particularly ungrateful in them in consequence of the gentleman-like usage which the British imprisoned officers met with in America; and thus we wearied ourselves, petitioning and remonstrating, but to no purpose at all; for General Massey, who commanded at Halifax, was as inflexible as the devil himself, a fine preparative this for Mr. Lovel, member of the Continental Congress.

Lieutenant Russell, whom I have mentioned before, came to visit me in prison, and assured me that he had done his utmost to procure my parole for enlargement; at which a British captain, who was then town-major, expressed compassion for the gentlemen confined in the filthy place, and assured me that he had used his influence to procure their enlargement; his name was near like Ramsey. Among the prisoners there were four in number who had a legal claim to a parole, a Mr. Howland, master of a continental armed vessel, a Mr. Taylor, his mate, and myself.

As to the article of provision, we were well served, much better than in any part of my captivity; and since it was Mr. Lovel's misfortune and mine to be prisoners, and in so wretched circumstances, I was happy that we were together as a mutual support to each other and to the unfortunate prisoners with us. Our first attention was

the preservation of ourselves and injured little republic; the rest of our time we devoted inter-
changeably to politics and philosophy, as patience
was a needful exercise in so evil a situation, but
contentment mean and impracticable.

I had not been in this jail many days, before a
worthy and charitable woman, by the name of
Mrs. Blacden, supplied me with a good dinner of
fresh meats every day, with garden fruit, and
sometimes with a bottle of wine; notwithstanding
which I had not been more than three weeks in
this place before I lost my appetite to the most
delicious food by the jail distemper, as also did
sundry of the prisoners, particularly Sergeant
Moore, a man of courage and fidelity. I have
several times seen him hold the boatswain of the
Solebay frigate, when he attempted to strike him,
and laughed him out of conceit of using him as a
slave.

A doctor visited the sick, and did the best, as I
suppose, he could for them, to no apparent purpose.
I grew weaker and weaker, as did the rest.
Several of them could not help themselves. At
last I reasoned in my own mind that raw onion
would be good. I made use of it, and found immediate relief by it, as did the sick in general,
particularly Sergeant Moore, whom it recovered
almost from the shades; though I had met with a
little revival, still I found the malignant hand of
Britain had greatly reduced my constitution with
stroke upon stroke. Esquire Lovel and myself

11

used every argument and entreaty that could be well conceived of in order to obtain gentleman-like usage, to no purpose. I then wrote General Massey as severe a letter as I possibly could with my friend Lovel's assistance. The contents of it was to give the British, as a nation, and him as an individual, their true character. This roused the rascal, for he could not bear to see his and the nation's deformity in that transparent letter, which I sent him; he therefore put himself in a great rage about it, and showed the letter to a number of British officers, particularly to Captain Smith of the *Lark* frigate, who instead of joining with him in disapprobation commended the spirit of it; upon which General Massey said to him, do you take the part of a rebel against me? Captain Smith answered that he rather spoke his sentiments and there was a dissension in opinion between them. Some officers took the part of the general and others of the captain. This I was informed of by a gentleman who had it from Captain Smith.

In a few days after this, the prisoners were ordered to go on board of a man-of-war, which was bound for New York; but two of them were not able to go on board, and were left at Halifax; one died; and the other recovered. This was about the 12th of October, and soon after we had got on board, the captain sent for me in particular to come on the quarter deck. I went, not knowing that it was Captain Smith or his ship at that time,

and expected to meet the same rigorous usage I
had commonly met with and prepared my mind
accordingly; but when I came on deck, the captain
met me with his hand, welcomed me to his ship,
invited me to dine with him that day, and assured
me that I should be treated as a gentleman, and
that he had given orders that I should be treated
with respect by the ship's crew. This was so unexpected and sudden a transition that it drew tears
from my eyes which all the ill usage I had before
met with was not able to produce, nor could I at
first hardly speak, but soon recovered myself and
expressed my gratitude for so unexpected a favor;
and let him know that I felt anxiety of mind in
reflecting that his situation and mine was such
that it was not probable that it would ever be in
my power to return the favor. Captain Smith replied that he had no reward in view, but only
treated me as a gentleman ought to be treated;
he said this is a mutable world, and one gentleman never knows but it may be in his power to
help another. Soon after I found this to be the
same Captain Smith who took my part against
General Massey; but he never mentioned anything
of it to me, and I thought it impolite in me to in-
terrogate him as to any disputes which might
have arisen between him and the general on my
account, as I was a prisoner, and that it was at
his option to make free with me on that subject if
he pleased; and if he did not, I might take it for
granted that it would be unpleasing for me to

query about it, though I had a strong propensity
to converse with him on that subject.

I dined with the captain agreeable to his invitation, and oftentimes with the lieutenant, in the
gun-room, but in general ate and drank with my
friend Lovel and the other gentlemen who were
prisoners with me, where I also slept.

We had a little berth inclosed with canvas, between decks, where we enjoyed ourselves very
well, in hopes of an exchange; besides, our friends
at Halifax had a little notice of our departure and
supplied us with spirituous liquor, and many articles of provisions for the cost. Captain Burk,
having been taken prisoner, was added to our
company (he had commanded an American armed
vessel) and was generously treated by the captain
and all the officers of the ship, as well as myself.
We now had in all near thirty prisoners on board,
and as we were sailing along the coast, if I recollect right, off Rhode Island, Captain Burk, with
an under-officer of the ship, whose name I do not
recollect, came to our little berth, proposed to kill
Captain Smith and the principal officers of the
frigate and take it; adding that there were thirty-
five thousand pounds sterling in the same. Captain Burk likewise averred that a strong party out
of the ship's crew was in the conspiracy, and urged
me, and the gentleman that was with me, to use
our influence with the private prisoners to execute
the design, and take the ship with the cash into
one of our own ports.

Upon which I replied that we had been too well used on board to murder the officers; that I could by no means reconcile it to my conscience, and that, in fact, it should not be done; and while I was yet speaking my friend Lovel confirmed what I had said, and farther pointed out the ungratefulness of such an act; that it did not fall short of murder, and in fine all the gentlemen in the berth opposed Captain Burk and his colleague. But they strenuously urged that the conspiracy would be found out, and that it would cost them their lives, provided they did not execute their design. I then interposed spiritedly and put an end to further argument on the subject, and told them that they might depend upon it upon my honor that I would faithfully guard Captain Smith's life. If they should attempt the assault I would assist him, for they desired me to remain neuter, and that the same honor that guarded Captain Smith's life would also guard theirs; and it was agreed by those present not to reveal the conspiracy, to the intent that no man should be put to death, in consequence of what had been projected; and Captain Burk, and his colleague went to stifle the matter among their associates. I could not help calling to mind what Captain Smith said to me, when I first came on board: "This is a mutable world, and one gentleman never knows but that it may be in his power to help another." Captain Smith and his officers still behaved with their usual courtesy, and I never heard any more of the conspiracy.

We arrived before New York, and cast anchor the latter part of October, where we remained several days, and where Captain Smith informed me that he had recommended me to Admiral Howe and General Sir William Howe, as a gentleman of honor and veracity, and desired that I might be treated as such. Captain Burk was then ordered on board a prison ship in the harbor. I took my leave of Captain Smith and, with the other prisoners, was sent on board a transport ship which lay in the harbor, commanded by Captain Craige, who took me into the cabin with him and his lieutenant. I fared as they did, and was in every respect well treated, in consequence of directions from Captain Smith. In a few weeks after this I had the happiness to part with my friend Lovel, for his sake, whom the enemy affected to treat as a private; he was a gentleman of merit, and liberally educated, but had no commission; they maligned him on account of his unshaken attachment to the cause of his country. He was exchanged for a Governor Philip Skene of the British. I was continued in this ship till the latter part of November, where I contracted an acquaintance with a captain of the British; his name has slipped my memory. He was what we may call a genteel, hearty fellow. I remember an expression of his over a bottle of wine, to this import: "That there is a greatness of soul for personal friendship to subsist between you and me, as we are upon opposite sides, and may at another

day be obliged to face each other in the field." I
am confident that he was as faithful as any officer
in the British army. At another sitting he offered
to bet a dozen of wine that Fort Washington
would be in the hands of the British in three days.
I stood the bet, and would, had I known that that
would have been the case; and the third day afterward we heard a heavy cannonade, and that day
the fort was taken sure enough. Some months
after, when I was on parole, he called upon me
with his usual humor, and mentioned the bet. I
acknowledged that I had lost it, but he said he
did not mean to take it, then, as I was a prisoner;
that he would another day call upon me, when
their army came to Bennington. I replied that he
was quite too generous, as I had fairly lost it; besides, the Green Mountain Boys would not suffer
them to come to Bennington. This was all in good
humor. I should have been glad to have seen
him after the defeat at Bennington, but did not.
It was customary for a guard to attend the prisoners, which was often changed. One was composed of tories from Connecticut, in the vicinity
of Fairfield and Green Farms. The sergeant's
name was Hoit. They were very full of their in-
vectives against the country, swaggered of their
loyalty to their king, and exclaimed bitterly
against the "cowardly Yankees," as they were
pleased to term them, but finally contented themselves with saying that when the country was
overcome they should be well rewarded for their

loyalty out of the estates of the whigs, which would be confiscated. This I found to be the general language of the tories, after I arrived from England on the American coast. I heard sundry of them relate, that the British generals had engaged them an ample reward for their losses, disappointments and expenditures, out of the forfeited rebels' estates. This language early taught me what to do with tories' estates, as far as my influence can go. For it is really a game of hazard between whig and tory. The whigs must inevitably have lost all, in consequence of the abilities of the tories, and their good friends the British; and it is no more than right the tories should run the same risk, in consequence of the abilities of the whigs. But of this more will be observed in the sequel of this narrative.

Some of the last days of November the prisoners were landed at New York, and I was admitted to parole with the other officers, viz.: Proctor, Howland, and Taylor. The privates were put into filthy churches in New York, with the distressed prisoners that were taken at Fort Washington; and the second night, Sergeant Roger Moore, who was bold and enterprising, found means to make his escape with every one of the remaining prisoners that were taken with him, except three, who were soon after exchanged. So that out of thirty-one prisoners, who went with me the round exhibited in these sheets, two only died with the enemy, and three only were exchanged; one of whom died after he came within our lines; all the rest, at different times, made their escape from the enemy.

I now found myself on parole, and restricted to the limits of the city of New York, where I soon projected means to live in some measure agreeably to my rank, though I was destitute of cash. My constitution was almost worn out by such a long and barbarous captivity. The enemy gave out that I was crazy, and wholly unmanned, but my vitals held sound, nor was I delirious any more than I had been from youth up; but my extreme circumstances, at certain times, rendered it politic to act in some measure the madman; and in consequence of a regular diet and exercise, my blood recruited, and my nerves in a great measure recovered their former tone, strength and usefulness, in the course of six months.

CHAPTER XIV.

ALLEN'S narrative in the preceding chapter gives a picture of himself, of the times,
and of the treatment of prisoners by the most
civilized nation on earth. In January, 1777,
with other American officers, he was quartered
on Long Island. In August he was sent to
the provost jail in New York. May 3, 1778,
he was exchanged for Col. Alexander Campbell. Thus he was treated as a colonel, although he had no fixed official rank or title
beyond that informally bestowed on him by
Montgomery. He was entertained with gentlemanly courtesy for two days at General
Campbell's headquarters on Staten Island, and
then crossed New Jersey amid the acclama-
tions of the people.

For several days he was the guest of Washington at Valley Forge. Here, eighteen miles
northwest of Philadelphia, where the British

army was revelling in luxury, Washington, with three thousand men suffering from cold and hunger, was praying to God for guidance in so sore a strait. Baron Steuben was there fresh from the service of Frederic the Great, disciplining the raw recruits into veteran soldiers never again to know defeat. There were Gates, attending a court-martial, and Putnam and Lafayette. These were among Allen's red-letter days; courteously entertained by some of the best soldiers of Europe and America, and the favored guest of Washington, could Heaven reward him better for his long imprisonment? Here he writes a letter to Congress which Washington forwards inclosed with his own. Allen began the journey to his Vermont home in company with Gates, arriving in Fishkill on May 18, and in Bennington just four weeks after his release from prison.

We now come to a chapter in Allen's life which the biographer must enter upon with a mind free from prejudice, and with a strong desire to assimilate the feelings of the age when our little commonwealth was in process of formation. About the close of the year 1776, Allen being a prisoner on parole in

New York, a British officer of rank sent for him to come to his lodgings. He told him that his fidelity, although in a wrong cause, had recommended him to General Sir William Howe, who wished to make him the colonel of a regiment of tories. He proposed that Allen in a few days should go to England, be paid in gold instead of continental rag money, be introduced to Lord George Germaine and probably to the king, return to America with Burgoyne, assist in reducing the country, and receive a large tract of land in Vermont or Connecticut as he preferred. Allen replied: "If by fidelity I have recommended myself to General Howe, I shall be loath by unfaithfulness to lose the general's good opinion; besides, I view the offer of land to be similar to that which the devil offered our Saviour, 'to give him all the kingdoms of the world to fall down and worship him,' when the poor devil had not one foot of land on earth."

Mr. B. F. Stevens, an American resident of London, and an indefatigable collector of documents relating to early American history gathered from the British archives, furnishes a letter written by Alexander C. Wedderburn, solicitor-general, on the morning of December

27, 1775, to William Eden, under-secretary of state. On the same day at noon a cabinet meeting was to be held at which was to be considered the disposition to be made of Ethan Allen and other prisoners who had reached England five days before. The "Lord S." referred to is Lord Suffolk, secretary of state, and the "Attorney" is Lord Edward Therlow, attorney-general:

DEAR EDEN:—I shall certainly attend Lord S. at 12 o'clock. My idea of the Business does not differ much from the Attorney's. My thoughts have been employed upon it ever since I saw you, and I am persuaded some unlucky incident must arise if Allen and his People are kept here. It must be understood that Government does not mean to execute them, the Prosecution will be re-miss and the Disposition of some People to thwart it very active. I would therefore send them back, · but I think something more might be done than merely to return them as Prisoners to America. Allen, by Kay's [William Kay, secret service agent at Montreal] account, took up arms because he was dispossessed of Lands he had settled between Hampshire and New York, in consequence of an order of Council settling the boundary of these two provinces, and had balanced for some time wheth-er to have recourse to ye Rebels or to Mr. Carle-ton [governor-general of the Province of Quebec].

The doubt of being well received by the latter determined him to join the former, and Kay adds that he is a bold, active fellow. I would then send to him a Person of Confidence with this Proposal: that his case had been favorably represented to Government; that the injury he had suffered was some Alleviation for his crime, and that it arose from an Abuse of an order of Council which was never meant to dispossess the Settlers in the Lands in debate between ye two provinces. If he has a mind to return to his duty He may not only have his pardon from Gen. Howe but a Company of Rangers, and in the event if He behaves well His lands restored on these terms, he and his men shall be sent back to Boston at liberty; if he does not accept them he and they must be disposed of as the Law directs. If he should behave well it is an Acquisition. If not there is still an Advantage in finding a decent reason for not immediately proceeding against him as a Rebel. Some of the People who came over in the Ship with him, or perhaps Kay himself, might easily settle this bargain if it is set about directly.

Yours ever,   A. C. W.

A correspondent of the Burlington *Free Press*, January 7, 1887, adds this comment:

That it was agreed to in the cabinet appears in the fact that on the very 27th December, 1775, Lord George Germaine of the admiralty ordered that Allen and his associates be returned to General

Howe in Boston. Howe evacuated Boston March
16, 1776, went to Halifax, and thence to New
York. Allen followed him round and was ulti-
mately a prisoner on parole until the 6th of May,
1778, when he was exchanged for Col. Archibald
Campbell. While he was on parole the " Person
of Confidence" was found to make the proposal
suggested by Wedderburn, and Allen mentions
this in the narrative of his captivity.

Who was the British officer of high rank
whom Howe employed to buy up Allen we do
not know, but the American whom Clinton
employed we do know: Beverly Robinson, a
Virginian, made wealthy by marriage with
Susanna Phillipse, sister of Mary Phillipse, for
whom Washington had an attachment. He
was the son of a lieutenant-governor, and an
early associate of Washington. In 1780 occurred this third attempt to buy Allen. Robinson was the man selected to make the proposition. Ethan Allen was the man selected
to be bribed: not Governor Chittenden; not
the soldiers Roger Enos or Seth Warner; not
the diplomat, the treasurer, the financier of the
State, Ira Allen; not the young lawyers Nathaniel Chipman or S. R. Bradley; but the man
who had been tempted in England and tempted

in New York, the man whose loyalty had not been shaken by the endurance of British brutality for two and one-half years. The time to hope for success would seem to have been December, 1775, on English soil, when he had reasonable grounds to fear being hung for treason, or in New York, in 1777, when Washington had been driven out of Long Island, out of New York City, and chased across New Jersey. This time chosen was in 1780, when Congress had alienated Vermont by ignoring her claims to federation, and had treated her with such contempt that there was almost no hope of her joining the United States.

Long Island knew of Ethan's temptation before he did. The air was full of it. The contents of Robinson's letter were known to the tories before Allen received it. The letter written in February was delivered in July. Washington heard in July that Allen was in New York selling himself to the British. Schuyler had spies everywhere. They reported Allen in Canada. General James Clinton suspected Allen. The correspondence and flag for cartel smelt of treason. Washington had tried to effect an exchange of prisoners and failed. His letter to Haldimand was unanswered. Gooch had applied, in July, to Washington, and Allen wrote to Washington at the request of the governor. Washington replied he could not prefer Warner's men to those who had been prisoners longer, but here the correspondence languished.

In the *Magazine of American History*, published in New York, January, 1887, is an article entitled " A Curious Chapter in Vermont's History," dated Ottawa, Canada, November, 1886, signed J. L. Payne, in which the writer says there are hundreds of manuscripts in the Canadian archives which prove that Vermont narrowly escaped becoming a British province. The chief evidence that he furnishes is extracts from the letters of Capt. Justus Sherwood, commissioner for General Haldimand, Governor of Canada. These letters indicate that on October 26, 1780, Sherwood left Miller Bay with five privates, a flag, drum, and fife. On October 28th he is at Herrick's Camp, a Vermont frontier post of three hundred men. He is blindfolded and taken to Colonel Herrick's room. He tells Herrick that he is sent by Major Carleton to negotiate a cartel for the exchange of prisoners, and that he had dispatches from Governor Haldimand

12

and Major Carleton to Governor Chittenden and Governor Allen. Next Sherwood is at Allen's headquarters in Castleton, and Allen having promised absolute secrecy, Sherwood informs him that:

General Haldimand was no stranger to their disputes with the other States respecting jurisdiction, and that his excellency was perfectly well informed of all that had lately passed between congress and Vermont, and of the fixed intentions of congress never to consent to Vermont's being a separate State. General Haldimand felt that in this congress was only duping them, and waited for a favorable opportunity to crush them; and therefore it was proper for them to cast off the congressional yoke and resume their former allegiance to the king of Great Britain, by doing which they would secure to themselves those privileges they had so long contended for with New York.

Allen is reported by Sherwood as replying that he was attached to the interests of Vermont, and that nothing but the continued tyranny of Congress could drive him from allegiance to the United States; but "Should he have any proposals to make to General Haldimand hereafter, they would be nearly as follows: He will expect to command his own forces. Vermont must be a government separate from and independent of any other Province in America; must chose their own officers and civil representatives; be entitled to all the privileges of the other states offered by the King's commissioners, and the New Hampshire Grants as chartered by Benning Wentworth, Governor of New Hampshire, must be confirmed free from any patents or claims from New York or other Provinces. He desires me to inform His Excellency that a revolution of this nature must be the work of time. . . . If, however, Congress should grant Vermont a seat in that Assembly as a separate State, then this negotiation to be at an end and be kept secret on both sides."

On May 7, 1781, Ira Allen visited Canada, and concerning a conference with him Captain Sherwood reports to the governor:

He says matters are not yet ripe. Governor Chittenden, General Allen and the major part of the leading men are anxious to bring about a neutrality, and are fully convinced that Congress never intends to confirm them as a separate State; but they dare not at this time make any separate agreement with Great Britain until the populace are better modelled for the purpose.

A few days later Captain Sherwood reports
to the governor:

Those suspicious circumstances, with the great
opinion Allen [referring to Col. Ira Allen] seems
to entertain of the mighty power and consequence
of Vermont, induce me to think they flatter themselves with the belief that, if Britain should invade them, the neighboring colonies rather than
lose them as a frontier would protect them, and,
on the other hand, should congress invade them,
they could easily be admitted to a union with
Britain at the latest hour, which they would at
the last extremity choose as the least of two evils;
for Allen says they hate congress like the devil,
and have not yet a very good opinion of Britain.
Sometimes I am inclined, from Allen's discourse,
to hope and almost believe that they are endeavoring to prepare for a reunion.   To this I suppose
I am somewhat inclined by my anxious desire that
it may be so.

Upon Col. Ira Allen's return to Vermont,
Captain Sherwood reports:

I believe Allen has gone with a full determi-
nation to do his utmost for a reunion, and I believe
he will be seconded by Governor Chittenden, his
brother Ethan Allen and a few others, all acting
from interest, without any principle of loyalty.

CHAPTER XV.

VERMONT'S TREATMENT BY CONGRESS.—ALLEN'S LET-
TERS TO COLONEL WEBSTER AND TO CONGRESS.—
REASONS FOR BELIEVING ALLEN A PATRIOT.

THE conduct of Congress in asking New
York, Massachusetts, and New Hampshire to
empower it to settle Vermont, without allowing her to act as a party but allowing her to
look on, dallying and postponing the measure
indefinitely, indicated New York's control of
Congress, and, as might have been expected,
Vermont's prowess and pluck would not submit to organic annihilation without a fight.
The British, under advice from home, might
easily strive to take advantage of the bitter
feelings engendered. Congress was struggling
with the question of the ownership of western
lands. Virginia and New York claimed almost all, the former by virtue of Clarke's con-
quests and the latter by purchase of the Iro-
quois, both shadowy, attenuated claims. The
smaller States wanted Vermont in the Union

to vote against these claims. Ethan Allen's letters, showing the turmoil of feeling in Vermont, as well as his own patriotism, have often been quoted.

To Colonel Webster he wrote:

SIR:—Last evening I received a flag from Major Carleton commanding the British forces at Crown Point, with proposals from General Haldimand, commander-in-chief in Canada, for settling a cartel for the exchange of prisoners. Major Carleton has pledged his faith that no hostilities shall be committed on any posts or scouts within the limits of this state during the negotiation. Lest your state [New York] should suffer an incursion in the interim of time, I have this day dispatched a flag to Major Carleton, requesting that he extend cessation of hostilities on the northern parts and frontiers of New York. You will therefore conduct your affairs as to scouts, &c., only on the defensive until you hear further from me.

I am, &c.,　　　ETHAN ALLEN.

To Colonel Webster. To be communicated to Colonel Williams and the posts on your frontier.

He also wrote to Colonel Webster:

RUPERT, about break of day
of the 31st October, 1780.

SIR:—Maj. Ebenezer Allen who commands at Pittsford has sent an express to me at this place, informing me that one of his scouts at 1 or 2 o'clock P.M. on the 29th instant, from Chimney Point, discovered four or five ships and gun-boats and batteaux, the lake covered and black, all making sail to Ticonderoga, skiffs flying to and from the vessels to the batteaux giving orders, and the foregoing quoted from the letter verbatim. But I cannot imagine that Major Carleton will violate his truce. I have sent Major Clarke with a flag to Major Carleton, particularly to confirm the truce on my part, and likewise to intercede in behalf of the frontiers of New York. What the motion of the British may be, or their design, I know not. You must judge for yourself. I send out scouts to further discover the object of the enemy. Maj. [Ebenezer] Allen thinks they have a design against your state.

From your humble servant,

ETHAN ALLEN.

He wrote to the president of Congress:

SUNDERLAND, 9 March, 1781.

SIR:—Inclosed I transmit your excellency two letters which I received under the signature thereto annexed, that they may be laid before congress. Shall make no comments on them, but submit the disposal of them to their consideration. They are the identical and only letters I ever received from him, and to which I have never returned any manner of answer, nor have I ever had

the least personal acquaintance with him, directly
or indirectly.   The letter of the 2d February,
1781, I received a few days afore with a duplicate
of the other, which I received the latter part of
July last past, in the high road in Arlington,
which I laid before Governor Chittenden and a
number of other principal gentlemen of the state
(within ten minutes after I received it) for advice;
the result, after mature deliberation, and considering the extreme circumstances of the state, was to
take no further notice of the matter.   The reasons
of such a procedure are very obvious to people of
this state, when they consider that congress has
previously claimed an exclusive right of arbitrat-
ing on the existence of Vermont as a separate
government.   New York, New Hampshire and
Massachusetts Bay at the same time claiming this
territory, either in whole or in part, and exerting
their influence to make schisms among the citizens,
thereby in a considerable degree weakening this
government and exposing its inhabitants to the
incursions of the British troops and their savage
allies from the province of Quebec.   It seems
that those governments, regardless of Vermont's
contiguous situation to Canada, do not consider
that their northern frontiers have been secured by
her, nor of the merit of this state in a long and
hazardous war, but have flattered themselves with
the expectation that this state could not fail (their
help) to be desolated by a foreign enemy, and that
their exorbitant claims and avaricious designs may

at some future period take place in this district of country. Notwithstanding those complicated embarrassments, and I might add discouragements, Vermont during the last campaign defended her frontiers, and at the close of it opened a truce with General Haldimand (who commands the British troops in Canada) in order to settle a cartel for the mutual exchange of prisoners, which continued near four weeks in the same situation, during which time Vermont secured the northern frontiers of her own, and that of the state of New York in consequence of my including the latter in the truce, although that government could have but little claim to my protection. I am confident that congress will not dispute my sincere attachment to the cause of my country, though I do not hesitate to say I am fully grounded in opinion that Vermont has indubitable right to agree on terms of cessation of hostilities with Great Britain, provided the United States persist in rejecting her application for a union with them, for Vermont of all people would be the most miserable were she obliged to defend the independence of United States and they at the same time claiming full liberty to overturn and ruin the independence of Vermont. I am persuaded when congress considers the circumstances of this state, they will be more surprised that I have transmitted them the inclosed letters than that I have kept them in custody so long, for I am as resolutely determined to defend the independence of Vermont, as congress are that of the United States, and, rather than fail, will retire with hardy Green Mountain Boys into the desolate caverns of the mountains and wage war with human nature at large.

(Signed)   ETHAN ALLEN.

His Excellency Samuel Huntingdon, Esq., Pres. of Congress.

Allen wrote to General Schuyler:

BENNINGTON, May 15, 1781.

A flag which I sent last fall to the British commanding officer at Crown Point, and which was there detained near one month, on their return gave me to understand that they [the British], at several different times, threatened to captivate your own person: said that it had been in their power to take some of your family the last campaign [during Carleton's invasion in October, 1780, probably], but that they had an eye to yourself. I must confess that such conversation before my flag seems rather flummery than real premeditated design. However, that there was such conversation I do not dispute, which you will make such improvement of as you see fit. I shall conclude with assuring your honor, that notwithstanding the late reports, or rather surmises of my corresponding with the enemy to the prejudice of the United States, it is wholly without foundation.

I am, sir, with due respect, your honor's obedient and humble servant,

ETHAN ALLEN.

To General Schuyler.

The following letter, believed by some people to have been written by Allen to General Haldimand, June 16, 1782, though unsigned, contains what is considered by his traducers damning evidence:

SIR:—I have to acquaint your excellency that I had a long conference with . . . [a British agent] last night. He tells me that through the channel of A [Sherwood] he had to request me in your name to repair to the shipping on Lake Champlain, to hold a personal conference with his [your] excellency. But as the bearer is now going to get out of my house to repair to his excellency, and would have set out yesterday had not the intelligence of the arrival of . . . postponed it until to-day. I thought it expedient to wait your excellency reconsidering the matter, after discussing the peculiar situation of both the external and internal policy of this state with the gentleman who will deliver this to you, and shall have, by the time your excellency has been acquainted with the state of the facts now existing, time to bring about a further and more extended connection in favor of the British interest which is now working at the general assembly at Windsor, near the Connecticut River. The last refusal of congress to admit this state into union has done more to awaken the common people to a sense of that interest and resentment of their conduct than all which they had done before. By their own ac-

count, they declare that Vermont does not and
shall not belong to their confederacy. The consequence is, that they may fight their own battles.
It is liberty which they say they are after, but will
not extend it to Vermont. Therefore Vermont
does not belong either to the confederacy or the
controversy, but are a neutral republic. All the
frontier towns are firm with these gentlemen in
the present administration of government, and,
to speak within bounds, they have a clear majority
of the rank and file in their favor. I am, etc.

N. B.—If it should be your excellency's pleasure,
after having conversed with the gentleman who
will deliver these lines, that I should wait on your
excellency at any part of Lake Champlain, I will
do it, except I should find that it would hazard my
life too much. There is a majority in congress,
and a number of the principal officers of the continental army continually planning against me. I
shall do everything in my power to render this
state a British province.

Ira Allen, that shrewd politician, says of the
letter:

This we consider a political proceeding to prevent the British forces from invading this State.

Our reasons for believing Ethan Allen always a patriot are:

First. His known faithfulness to the American cause in every case.

Second. His hatred of the British and contemptuous rejection of their proffers of honor and emoluments when in their power and in no personal danger if he accepted them.

Third. His natural obstinacy in clinging to a cause he had espoused.

Fourth. The repeated efforts of the Vermont government, in which Allen was engaged, to induce Congress to admit it to the Union continued during the negotiation.

Fifth. At Allen's request the truce offered by the British included New York's eastern frontier, and Vermont promptly responded to all calls upon her for help.

Sixth. There is reason to believe that General Washington was informed by General Allen, in advance of the Haldimand negotiations, of their purpose.

The state's peculiar frontier, threatened by Canada, unsupported by the other states, disturbed by internal dissensions, unable to defend herself by force, made it necessary to use strategy. No authority was given the commissioners by the executive or by the legislature to treat of anything but an exchange of prisoners. There is no record that I can find that an effort was made at any time to induce Vermonters at large to consider the subject of a British union. Indeed, Governor Chittenden, in 1793, giving a list of those in the secret, mentions only eight, although Ira Allen said, in 1781, that more were added.

It seems to me that Allen shows in this correspondence the talent of a diplomat, a talent which our state needed in its formative period to supplement the audacity of the hardy Green Mountain Boys. There could be no question of disloyalty to the United States, because Vermont had never belonged to them. He was intensely loyal to his own state, for whose welfare he strove, and if Congress still refused to admit her to the Union, there was no other resource than to ally her with Great Britain in self-defence.

CHAPTER XVI.

WHEN Allen bade adieu to Washington at
Valley Forge, he rode on horseback to Fishkill with General Gates and suite, arriving at
that place on the 18th of May, 1778, the very
day his brother Heman died at Salisbury.
The six or eight days occupied by the trip
across New Jersey seems to have been one of
unalloyed enjoyment to the hero of Ticonderoga.   He tells us that Gates treated him with
the generosity of a lord and the freedom of a
boon companion.   That this intercourse impressed Gates favorably with Allen his correspondence with General Stark later demon-
strates.   On Sunday evening, the 31st of May,
Allen arrived at Bennington.   The town being orthodox and Congregationalist, Sunday is
observed with Puritanic severity, but he finds

the people too jubilant for religious solemnity. The old iron six-pound cannon from Fort Hoosac is brought out and fired in honor of the new state of Vermont.

What changes have taken place during his three years' absence! His only son is dead; his wife and four daughters are in Sunderland; two brothers have become state officers. Levi Allen, one of the foremost Green Mountain Boys in 1775, has now become a tory. Burgoyne has swept along the western borders and has been captured. Allen's old followers, under Seth Warner, have won renown at Quebec, Montreal, Hubbardston, Bennington, Saratoga, and Ticonderoga. The constitution has been formed and the state government organized. A legislature has been elected, held one session, and adjourned to meet again this week.

One of the great spectacles of the Anglo-Saxon civilization had been appointed for this time and place. A criminal, David Redding, convicted of treason, was to be executed. Upon a petition for rehearing on the ground that he had been convicted by a jury of only six men, the governor had reprieved Redding until Thursday, the 11th. The news of the

reprieve, noised through the town, called together a disappointed and angry crowd, in the
midst of which Allen appeared, mounted a
stump, and cried: "Attention, the whole!"
He then expressed his sympathy with the people, explained the illegality of the trial, and
told them to go home and return in a week,
and they "shall see a man hung; if not Redding, I will be," and the appeased crowd peace-
ably dispersed. In the next trial Allen was
appointed state's attorney to prosecute Redding, who was condemned.

Soon Allen's attention is called to the controversy between New York and Vermont.
In the preceding February, after the constitution was adopted, before the government
was inaugurated, Governor Clinton, of New
York, issued a proclamation ostentatious with
apparent clemency and generosity. Ethan
Allen was selected as the proper man to expose the pompous fraud. Clinton began by
saying that the disaffection existing in Vermont was partially justified by the atrocious
acts of the British government while New
York was a colony, the act of outlawry which
sentenced Allen and others to death without
trial, the fees and unjust preference in grants

13

to servants of the crown over honest settlers, and he offered to discharge all claims under the outlawry act, to reduce the New York quit-rents to the New Hampshire rate, to make the fees of patents reasonable, and to confirm all grants made by New Hampshire and Massachusetts.

Allen replied, in a pamphlet, that the British act of outlawry had been dead by its own provision two and a half years, no thanks to Clinton; that most of the grants of New Hampshire and Massachusetts had been covered by New York patents, and that, as a matter of law, it was impossible for New York to cancel her former patents and confirm the New Hampshire grants, and he cited the opinion of the lords of trade to that effect.

But Vermont was in a dangerous position in reference to New Hampshire. A portion of that state had seceded and united with Vermont. The two states had fought side by side, but now New Hampshire had become unfriendly and remained so for years. The governor and council, perplexed with the difficulty, appointed Allen an agent to visit Congress and ask for advice. This is his first embassy from Vermont to Congress. He reported that "unless the union with New Hampshire towns is dissolved the nation will annihilate Vermont."

His second embassy was with Jonas Fay, in 1779, to inform Congress of the progress of affairs in Vermont.

His third embassy was in 1780, when he was chosen by the legislature as the chairman of a very able and eminent committee, Stephen R. Bradley, Moses Robinson, Paul Spooner, and Jonas Fay, to act as counsel for Vermont before Congress against the ablest men of New York and New Hampshire.

In 1779 he was sent to the Massachusetts court with a letter from the governor asking for a statement of Massachusetts' claim to Vermont. The reply was that Massachusetts claimed west from the Merrimac, and three miles further north, to the Pacific. This included part of Vermont.

It is noteworthy that Allen was elected a member of the legislature from Arlington while his family lived in Sunderland, and he called Bennington his "usual home." It is notable, also, that the constitution required every member of the legislature to take an oath that he believed in the divine inspiration

of the Bible and professed the Protestant religion, an oath which Allen refused to take,
and yet was allowed to act as a member.

It was in 1778 that Allen complained to the
court of confiscation that his brother Levi had
become a tory; had passed counterfeit Continental money; that under pretence of helping
him while a prisoner on Long Island, he had
been detected in supplying the British with
provisions. He stated that Levi owned real
estate in Vermont and prayed that that estate
might be confiscated to the public treasury.
For this act Levi afterward challenged Ethan
to a duel, but Ethan took no notice of the challenge.

In the spring of 1779 the Yorkers in Windham County wrote to Governor Clinton that
unless New York aided them, "our persons
and property must be at the disposal of Ethan
Allen; which is more to be dreaded than death
with all its terrors."

In May the superior court sat at Westminster. Thirty-six Yorkers were in jail. Their
offence consisted in rescuing two cows from
an officer who had seized them because their
owners had refused to do military duty on the
frontier or to pay for substitutes. Ethan Al-

len was there by order of Governor Chittenden, with one hundred Green Mountain Boys,
to aid the court. Three prisoners were discharged for want of evidence, three more because they were minors. Allen, hearing of
this, entered the court-room in his military
dress, large three-cornered hat profusely orna-
mented with gold lace, and a large sword
swinging by his side. Breathless with haste,
he bowed to Chief Justice Robinson and began attacking the attorneys. Robinson told
him the court would gladly listen to him as a
citizen, but not as a military man in a military
dress. Allen threw his hat on the table and
unbuckled his sword, exclaiming: "For forms
of government let fools contest; whate'er is
best administered is best." Observing the
judges whispering together, he said: "I said
that fools might contest, not your honors, not
your honors." To the state's attorney, Noah
Smith, he said: "I would have the young gentleman know that with my logic and reasoning
from the eternal fitness of things, I can upset
his Blackstones, his whitestones, his grave-
stones, and his brimstones." Then he continued:

Fifty miles I have come through the woods with my brave men to support the civil with the military arm, to quell any disturbances should they arise, and to aid the sheriff and court in prosecuting these Yorkers, the enemies of our noble State. I see, however, that some of them, by the quirks of this artful lawyer, Bradley, are escaping from the punishment they so richly deserve, and I find also, that this little Noah Smith is far from understanding his business, since he at one moment moves for a prosecution and in the next wishes to withdraw it. Let me warn your honors to be on your guard lest these delinquents should slip through your fingers and thus escape the rewards so justly due their crimes.

Allen then put on his hat, buckled on his sword, and departed with great dignity.

CHAPTER XVII.

IN 1782 the rebellious York element in
Windham County again called Ethan to the
field. In Guilford forty-six men ambushed
and fired on Allen's party in the evening.
Allen, knowing the terror of his name, entering Guilford on foot, uttered this proclamation: "I, Ethan Allen, do declare that I will
give no quarter to the man, woman, or child
who shall oppose me, and unless the inhabitants of Guilford peacefully submit to the authority of Vermont, I swear that I will lay it
as desolate as Sodom and Gomorrah by God."

In 1784 Allen published a book entitled
" Reason, the Only Oracle of Man: or, A Com-
pendious System of Natural Religion." In
this book Allen endeavored to prove that the
Bible was not inspired, but he declared it a

necessity that a future life of rewards and pun-
ishments follow the good and evil of this life.
His idea of the Deity is expressed in these
words:

The knowledge of the being, perfections, cre-
ation and providence of God and·the immortality
of our souls is the foundation of our religion.

This book contained 487 pages. Fifteen
hundred copies were issued, but most of them
were destroyed by the burning of the printing
office. Allen wrote to a friend:

In this book you read my very soul, for I have
not concealed my opinion. I expect that the
clergy and their devotees will proclaim war with
me in the name of the Lord.

Sometimes Allen is too profane to be repeated, sometimes too frivolous for sacred subjects. Speaking of his prospects of being hung
in England, he said:

As to the world of spirits, though I know nothing of the mode or manner of it, I expected nevertheless, when I should arrive at such a world,
that I should be as well treated as other gentlemen of my merit.

Among the pleasant friends that Allen
formed at this time was John Stark. The

hero of Ticonderoga had never met the hero of Bennington. Three weeks after Allen's arrival in Bennington, Stark wrote to him proposing an interview at Albany, where he was stationed as brigadier-general in command of the northern department. He also wrote to General Gates:

I should be very glad to have Colonel Ethan Allen command in the grants, as he is a very suitable man to deal with tories and such like villains.

Four days later Gates wrote Stark:

I now inclose two letters, one to Colonel Ethan Allen and one to Colonel Bedel . . . it may not be amiss to take Colonel Allen's opinion on the subject, with whom I wish you to open a correspondence.

Another pleasant episode in Allen's life was his association with St. John de Crèvecœur, who was the French consul in New York for ten years following the revolution. Sieur Crèvecœur married an American Quakeress, bought a farm which he cleared, wrote a book in English called "Letters from an American Farmer," and three volumes in French about upper Pennsylvania and New York. He wrote to Ethan Allen proposing to have the Vermont state seal engraved in silver by the king's best engravers, asked for maps of the state, suggested naming some towns after French statesmen who had befriended America. (St. Johnsbury was named for Crèvecœur.) He asked Allen for copies of his "Oracles of Reason" and also for some seeds.

Instances multiply showing the prominence of Ethan Allen in the new state. During Shay's rebellion in Massachusetts, before attempting to seize the United States arsenal at Springfield, he sent two of his principal officers to Ethan Allen offering to him the command of the Massachusetts insurgents, representing one-third of the population of that state. Allen rejected the offer with contempt and ordered the messengers to leave the state. He also wrote to the governor of Massachusetts and Colonel Benjamin Simmons, of western Massachusetts, informing them of the efforts made in Vermont by malcontents from that state, and that Vermont was exerting herself vigorously to prevent the evil consequences of the insurgents' action, and promising the most cordial co-operation in the future.

The incidents of Allen's life and his writings are not published in any one volume, but are scattered through ill-bound primers, are found in fiction, in addresses, and in huge double-column tomes which are not accessible to the people.

The story of his second marriage gives a vivid picture of the rough-and-ready audacious soldier. On the 9th of February, 1784, the judges of the supreme court were at break-fast with lawyer Stephen R. Bradley, of West-minster, when General Allen, in a sleigh with a span of dashing black horses and a colored driver, drove up to the house. Passing through the breakfast-room, he found in the next room the spirited young widow of twenty-four sum-mers, Mrs. Frances Buchanan, who was living in the house with her mother, Mrs. Wall. Dressed in her morning gown, Mrs. Buchanan was standing on a chair arranging china and glass on some upper shelves. She amused her visitor with some witticism about the broken decanter in her hands; a brief chat ensued, then Allen said: "Fanny, if we are ever to be married, now is the time, for I am on my way to Arlington."

"Very well," she replied; "give me time to put on my josie."

The couple passed into a third room, where the judges were smoking, and Allen said:

"Judge Robinson, this young woman and myself have concluded to marry each other, and to have you perform the ceremony."

"When?"

"Now! For myself I have no great opinion of such formality, and from what I can discover she thinks as little of it as I do. But as a decent respect for the opinion of mankind seems to require it, you will proceed."

"General, this is an important matter, and have you given it serious consideration?"

"Certainly; but," here the general glanced proudly at his handsome and accomplished bride, twenty-two years younger than himself, perhaps also conscious of his own mature, stalwart symmetry, "I do not think it requires much consideration in this particular case."

"Do you promise to live with Frances agreeably to the law of God?"

"Stop! stop!" cried Allen, looking out of the window. "Yes, according to the law of God as written in the great book of Nature. Go on! go on! my team is at the door."

Soon the bride's guitar and trunk were in

the sleigh and the bells jingled merrily as they dashed westward.

Before his second marriage John Norton, a tavern-keeper of Westminster, said:

"Fanny, if you marry General Allen you will be the queen of a new state."

"Yes," she replied, "and if I should marry the devil I would be queen of hell."

The children of the second marriage were three: one daughter who died in a nunnery in Montreal, and two sons who became officers in the United States Army and died at Norfolk, Va. Ethan Allen, of New York, is a grandson of the second wife.

CHAPTER XVIII.

DEATH.—CIVILIZATION IN ALLEN'S TIME.—ESTIMATES
OF ALLEN.—RELIGIOUS FEELING IN VERMONT.—
MONUMENTS.

IN 1787 Allen moved to Burlington, where, for the last two years of his life, he devoted himself to farming. Through a partial failure of the crops in 1789, Allen found himself short of hay in the winter. Col. Ebenezer Allen, who lived in South Hero, an island near Burlington, offered to supply Ethan what he needed if he would come for it. Accordingly, with a team and man, Ethan crossed the ice on the 10th of February. Col. Ebenezer Allen had invited some neighbors, who were old friends and acquaintances, to meet his guest, and the afternoon and evening were spent in telling stories. Ethan was persuaded to stay over night and the next morning started for home with his load of hay. During the journey his negro spoke to him several times but received no reply. On reaching home he discovered that his master was unconscious. He was carried into his house and died from apoplexy in a few hours.

To estimate properly Allen's force of character and large mind, we should appreciate the crude civilization of the early pioneer days of Vermont, when self-culture could only be procured by great qualities. The population was about five thousand, chiefly on the east side of the mountains. The bulk of the people lived in log houses with earthen floors, and with windows made of oiled paper, isinglass, raw hides, or sometimes 6 x 8 panes of glass. Smaller log houses were used to protect domestic animals from wolves and bears, as well as from the inclemency of the weather. It was the life of the frontier in the wilderness, when the struggle for bare sustenance left little time for the acquirement of knowledge, much less of accomplishments.

Allen is not the best representative man of his time, but his experience was so startling, his character so piquant, that a sketch of him better photographs Vermont before her admission to the Union than that of any other man. As a statesman he was infinitely inferior to Chipman or Bradley; as a soldier, Seth

Warner, although six years younger, was his superior; Ira Allen was more capable and more accomplished; Governor Chittenden was more discreet in the management of state affairs. As a captive, absent from the state from 1775 to 1778, Allen had nothing to do with the adoption of the constitution or the first organization of our state government; as a member of the legislature he won no reputation. He lacked the scholarly culture and polished suavity of the highest type of gentleman; he was sometimes horribly profane. He delighted in battling with the religious orthodoxy of New England; he wrote a book to disprove the authenticity of the Bible; yet he was energetic in his expressions of veneration for the being and perfection of the Deity, and a firm believer in the immortality of the soul. Thoroughly familiar with the history and law of the New York controversy, his telling exposure of the subtle casuistry of the more learned New York lawyers; his thorough sympathy with the settlers in all their trials and amusements; his geniality, sociability, and aptness in story-telling; his detestation of all dishonesty and meanness; his burning zeal for American freedom; his adroit success, his bitter sufferings, even his one unlucky rashness in attacking Montreal when deserted by the very man who had induced him to undertake it; his numerous writings—all combine to make him the most popular of our state characters.

Washington's masterly knowledge of human nature gives value to his brief portrait of Allen. Immediately on being released from captivity, Allen visited Washington at Valley Forge. Washington wrote to Congress in regard to Allen.

His fortitude and firmness seem to have placed him out of the reach of misfortune. There is an original something about him that commands admiration, and his long captivity and sufferings have only served to increase, if possible, his enthusiastic zeal. He appears very desirous of rendering his services to the states and of being employed, and at the same time he does not discover any ambition for high rank.

Senator Edmunds says of Allen: "Ethan Allen was a man of gifts rather than acquirements, although he was not by any means deficient in that knowledge obtained from reading and from intercourse with men. But it was the natural force of his character that made him eminent among the worthiest who

14

founded the republic, and pre-eminent among those who founded the state of Vermont."

Col. John A. Graham, who knew Allen well the last two or three years of his life, published a book in England a few years after Allen's death and therein says: "Ethan Allen was a man of extraordinary character. He possessed great talents but was deficient in education. In all his dealings he possessed the strictest sense of honor, integrity, and uprightness."

The Hon. Daniel P. Thompson attributes to him "wisdom, aptitude to command, ability to inspire respect and confidence, a high sense of honor, generosity, and kindness."

Jared Sparks calls him "brave, generous, consistent, true to his friends, true to his country, seeking at all times to promote the best interests of mankind."

Governor Hiland Hall says: "He acquired much information by reading and observation. His knowledge of the political situation of the state and country was general and accurate. As a writer, he was ready, clear, and forcible. His style attracted and fixed attention and inspired confidence in his sincerity and justice."

John Jay speaks of his writings as having "wit, quaintness, and impudence."

In financial skill Ethan was inferior to his brother Ira; as a soldier he lacked the cool judgment of Seth Warner; in administrative ability he had neither the tact nor success of Governor Chittenden; as a statesman he was destitute of the learning and ability of Chipman and Bradley; but as a patriot and friend he was true as a star. No money, no office, could bribe; no insults, no suffering, tame him. As a boon companion he was rollicking and popular. Many are the stories told of his hearty good-will toward all. One instance will show his power to attach the common people to him: Finding a woman in Tinmouth dreading to have a painful tooth drawn, in order to encourage her he sat down and had one of his perfectly sound teeth extracted.

In religion, like Horace Greeley, Allen had reverence for the Deity but none for the Bible. In this he was not alone, for Vermont, in the later eighteenth century, presented a curious mixture of the strictest adherence to the letter of the religious law and absolute free-thinking.

The Universalists in 1785 held their first American convention in Massachusetts. When this doctrine was first introduced into Ver-

mont, John Norton, the Westminster tavern-
keeper, said to Ethan Allen: "That religion
will suit you, will it not, General Allen?"

Allen, who knew Norton to be a secret tory,
replied in utter scorn: "No! no! for there
must be a hell in the other world for the punishment of tories."

President Dwight said: "Many of the influential early Vermonters were professed infi-
dels or Universalists, or persons of equally
loose principles and morals." Judge Robert
R. Livingston wrote Dr. Franklin: "The bulk
of Vermonters are New England Presbyterian
whigs." Daniel Chipman says: "Great numbers of the early settlers were of the set of
New-lights or Separates, who fled from perse-
cution in the New England States and found
religious liberty here."

Before Allen took Ticonderoga, Vermont
had eleven Congregational and four Baptist
churches. For a quarter of a century (1783–
1807) towns and parishes could assess taxes for
churches and ministers. At the very thresh-
old of Vermont's existence the laws had a Puritanic severity. "High-handed blasphemy"
was punished with death; while fines or the
stocks were the rewards of profane swearing,

drunkenness, unseasonable night-walking, disturbing Sabbath worship, travelling Sunday, gaming, horse-racing, confirmed tavern-haunting, mischievous lying, and even meeting in company Saturday or Sunday evenings except in religious meetings. "No person shall drive a team or droves of any kind, or travel on the Lord's day (except it be on business that concerns the present war, or by some adversity they are belated and forced to lodge in the woods, wilderness,·or highways the night before)," then only to next shelter. The wife of the Rev. Sam. Williams was arrested in New Hampshire for travelling on Sunday. No Jew, Roman Catholic, atheist, or deist could take the oath required of a member of the legislature; for that oath professed belief in the Deity, the divine inspiration of both Testaments, and the Protestant religion. The Rev. Samuel Peters, LL.D., sometimes called Bishop Peters, tells us the Munchausen story that he baptized into the Church of England 1,200 adults and children amid the forests of Vermont. In 1790 Vermont was enough of a diocese to hold a convention of eight parishes and two rectors.

Bennington was the early nucleus of Vermont colonization. Samuel Robinson, of that town, had land to sell both in Bennington and the adjoining town of Shaftsbury. It is said he entertained over night the new immigrants; if Baptists, he sold them land in Shaftsbury; if Congregationalists, he sold them land in Bennington.

What visible tokens have we of Vermont's pride in this hero, to whom she is so much indebted for her existence as a state?

The earliest statue of Ethan Allen was by Benjamin Harris Kinney, a native of Sunderland. It was modelled in Burlington and exhibited there in 1852. The Rev. Zadoc Thompson said of it: "All who have long and carefully examined his statue will admit that the artist, Mr. Kinney, our respected townsman, has embodied and presented to the eye the ideal in a most masterly manner." The Hon. David Read says: "The statue was examined by several aged people who had personally known Allen, and all pronounce it an excellent likeness of him." Henry de Puy has an engraving of this statue in his book about Allen in 1853. This statue has never been purchased from Mr. Kinney, and it is still in his possession.

The two statues of Allen made for the state are the work of Larkin G. Mead, a native of Chesterfield, N. H., reared and educated in Brattleboro. One of them, at the entrance of the state-house in Montpelier, is of Rutland marble. The other one, in the Capitol at Washington, is of Italian marble.

The fourth statue was unveiled at Burlington, the 4th of July, 1873. It was made at Carrara, Italy, after a design by Peter Stephenson, of Boston. It is 8 ft. 4 in. high, stands on a granite shaft 42 ft. in height, in Green Mountain Cemetery, on the banks of the Winooski.

" Siste viator! Heroa calcas!"

GOOD BOOKS FOR YOUNG READERS.

JOHN BOYD'S ADVENTURES. By THOMAS W. KNOX, author of "The Boy Travelers," etc. With 12 full-page Illustrations. 12mo. Cloth, $1.50.

"The hero is alternately merchant, sailor, man-o'-war's-man, privateer's-man, pirate, and Algerine slave. The bombardment of Tripoli is a brilliant chapter of a narrative of heroic deeds."—*Philadelphia Ledger.*

"We venture to assert that no boy who takes up the story of John Boyd will feel inclined to put it down until he has turned the last page."—*San Francisco Call.*

ALONG THE FLORIDA REEF. By CHARLES F. HOLDER, joint author of "Elements of Zoölogy." With numerous Illustrations. 12mo. Cloth, $1.50.

"The reader will be entertained with a series of adventures, but when he is done he will find that he has learned a good deal about dancing cranes, corals, waterspouts, sharks, talking fish, disappearing islands, hurricanes, turtles, and all sorts of wonders of the earth and sea and air."—*New York Sun.*

ENGLISHMAN'S HAVEN. By W. J. GORDON, author of "The Captain - General," etc. With 8 full-page Illustrations. 12mo. Cloth, $1.50.

"The story of Louisbourg, which because of its position and the consequences of its fall is justly held one of the most notable of the world's dead cities. The story is admirably told."—*Detroit Free Press.*

"Full of exciting adventure, battle, and siege. The hero is a brave young English boy who is with the soldiers at the fort."—*Chicago Times.*

WE ALL. A story of outdoor life and adventure in Arkansas. By OCTAVE THANET. With 12 full-page Illustrations by E. J. AUSTEN and others. 12mo. Cloth, $1.50.

"A story which every boy will read with unalloyed pleasure. . . . The adventures of the two cousins are full of exciting interest. The characters, both white and black, are sketched directly from nature, for the author is thoroughly familiar with the customs and habits of the different types of Southerners that she has so effectively reproduced."—*Boston Saturday Evening Gazette.*

KING TOM AND THE RUNAWAYS. By LOUIS PENDLETON. The experiences of two boys in the forests of Georgia. With 6 Illustrations by E. W. KEMBLE. 12mo. Cloth, $1.50.

"The doings of 'King' Tom, Albert, and the happy-go-lucky boy Jim on the swamp island, are as entertaining in their way as the old sagas embodied in Scandinavian story."—*Philadelphia Ledger.*

New York: D. APPLETON & CO., 72 Fifth Avenue.

MEMOIRS ILLUSTRATING THE HISTORY OF NAPOLEON I, from 1802 to 1815. By Baron CLAUDE-FRANÇOIS DE MÉNEVAL, Private Secretary to Napoleon. Edited by his Grandson, Baron NAPOLEON JOSEPH DE MÉNEVAL. With Portraits and Autograph Letters. In three volumes. 8vo. Cloth, $6.00.

These volumes furnish a picture of Napoleon's daily life which is believed to be unexcelled in point of closeness of observation and graphic detail by any other narrative. That Méneval was not the man to neglect his opportunities is shown abundantly by the glimpses of character revealed in his diaries and notes. Yet, for personal and other reasons, his invaluable recollections were not given to the world. They have been treasured by his family until the present time of profound interest in Napoleonic history. Of Napoleon's relations with Josephine and Marie Louise—of all the features of his domestic and social existence—Méneval had abundant knowledge, for he shared Napoleon's private life; and since he was sitting at the fountainhead of information, he is able to shed new light on many features of the Napoleonic campaigns. His narrative is most interesting; its historical importance need not be emphasized.

"The Baron de Méneval knew Napoleon as few knew him. He was his confidential secretary and intimate friend. . . . Students and historians who wish to form a trustworthy estimate of Napoleon can not afford to neglect this testimony by one of his most intimate associates."—*London News.*

"These memoirs, by the private secretary of Napoleon, are a valuable and important contribution to the history of the Napoleonic period, and necessarily they throw new and interesting light on the personality and real sentiments of the emperor. If Napoleon anywhere took off the mask, it was in the seclusion of his private cabinet. The memoirs have been republished almost as they were written, by Baron de Méneval's grandson, with the addition of some supplementary documents."—*London Times.*

"Méneval has brought the living Napoleon clearly before us in a portrait, flattering, no doubt, but essentially true to nature; and he has shown us what the emperor really was—at the head of his armies, in his Council of State, as the ruler of France, as the lord of the continent—above all, in the round of his daily life, and in the circle of family and home."—*London Academy.*

"Neither the editor nor translator of Méneval's memoirs has miscalculated his deep interest—an interest which does not depend on literary style but on the substance of what is related Whoever reads this volume will wait with impatience for the remainder."—*N. Y. Tribune.*

"The work will take rank with the most important of memoirs relating to the period. Its great value arises largely from its author's transparent veracity. Méneval was one of those men who could not consciously tell anything but the truth. He was constitutionally unfitted for lying. . . . The book is extremely interesting, and it is as important as it is interesting."—*N. Y. Times.*

"Few memoirists have given us a more minute account of Napoleon. . . . No lover of Napoleon, no admirer of his wonderful genius, can fail to read these interesting and important volumes which have been waited for for years."—*N. Y. World.*

"The book will be hailed with delight by the collectors of Napoleonic literature, as it covers much ground wholly unexplored by the great majority of the biographers of Napoleon."—*Providence Journal.*

New York: D. APPLETON & CO., 72 Fifth Avenue.

*A*BRAHAM LINCOLN : *The True Story of a Great LIFE.* By WILLIAM H. HERNDON and JESSE W. WEIK. With numerous Illustrations. New and revised edition, with an introduction by HORACE WHITE. In two volumes. 12mo. Cloth, $3.00.

This is probably the most intimate life of Lincoln ever written. The book, by Lincoln's law-partner, William H. Herndon, and his friend Jesse W. Weik, shows us Lincoln the man. It is a true picture of his surroundings and influences and acts. It is not an attempt to construct a political history, with Lincoln often in the background, nor is it an effort to apotheosize the American who stands first in our history next to Washington. The writers knew Lincoln intimately. Their book is the result of unreserved association. There is no attempt to portray the man as other than he really was, and on this account their frank testimony must be accepted, and their biography must take permanent rank as the best and most illuminating study of Lincoln's character and personality. Their story, simply told, relieved by characteristic anecdotes, and vivid with local color, will be found a fascinating work.

"Truly, they who wish to know Lincoln as he really was must read the biography of him written by his friend and law-partner, W. H. Herndon. This book was imperatively needed to brush aside the rank growth of myth and legend which was threatening to hide the real lineaments of Lincoln from the eyes of posterity. On one pretext or another, but usually upon the plea that he was the central figure of a great historical picture, most of his self-appointed biographers have, by suppressing a part of the truth and magnifying the rest, produced portraits which those of Lincoln's contemporaries who knew him best are scarcely able to recognize. There is, on the other hand, no doubt about the faithfulness of Mr. Herndon's delineation. The marks of unflinching veracity are patent in every line."—*New York Sun.*

"Among the books which ought most emphatically to have been written must be classed 'Herndon's Lincoln.'"—*Chicago Inter-Ocean.*

"The author has his own notion of what a biography should be, and it is simple enough. The story should tell all, plainly and even bluntly. Mr. Herndon is naturally a very direct writer, and he has been industrious in gathering material. Whether an incident happened before or behind the scenes, is all the same to him. He gives it without artifice or apology. He describes the life of his friend Lincoln just as he saw it."—*Cincinnati Commercial Gazette.*

"A remarkable piece of literary achievement—remarkable alike for its fidelity to facts, its fullness of details, its constructive skill, and its literary charm."—*New York Times.*

"It will always remain the authentic life of Abraham Lincoln."—*Chicago Herald.*

"The book is a valuable depository of anecdotes, innumerable and characteristic. It has every claim to the proud boast of being the 'true story of a great life.'"—*Philadelphia Ledger.*

"Will be accepted as the best biography yet written of the great President."—*Chicago Inter-Ocean.*

"Mr. White claims that, as a portraiture of the man Lincoln, Mr. Herndon's work 'will never be surpassed.' Certainly it has never been equaled yet, and this new edition is all that could be desired."—*New York Observer.*

"The three portraits of Lincoln are the best that exist ; and not the least characteristic of these, the Lincoln of the Douglas debates, has never before been engraved . . . Herndon's narrative gives, as nothing else is likely to give, the material from which we may form a true picture of the man from infancy to maturity."—*The Nation.*

New York : D. APPLETON & CO., 72 Fifth Avenue.